The
Great Gatsby
Murder Case

Books by David Finkle

People Tell Me Things

The Man With the Overcoat

Humpty Trumpty Hit a Brick Wall:
Donald J. Trump's First White House Year in Verse

Great Dates With Some Late Greats

Keys to an Empty House

The
Great Gatsby
Murder Case

David Finkle

Plum Bay Publishing, LLC
New York, New York
Morristown, New Jersey

For permission requests, contact the publisher at the website below
Plum Bay Publishing, LLC
www.plumbaypublishing.com

Library of Congress Control Number:
Paperback ISBN: 979-8-9858564-5-3
eBook ISBN: 979-8-9858564-7-7
Library of Congress Control Number: 2024904520

Printed in the United States of America

Cover Design: Jet Purdie
Interior Design: Barbara Aronica
Copyedited by Sally Fay

For Bess and Les

MONDAY

It's important to know I live in New York City—more specifically in Manhattan—which luckily remains a city of readers. Furthermore, it's a city of readers who…I won't say a city of readers who throw books out. Not at all. It's a city of readers often living in cramped quarters where they can't accommodate all their books. It's a city where readers put books in stacks or boxes on stoops or on the tops of trash cans so that other readers can search through them. What a great amenity: neighbors giving so openly, so generously and anonymously to neighbors, to strangers.

But even the best amenities have their downsides. Take, for example, what recently happened to me. I was walking down my street one morning, returning from the local Rite Aid, five-cent paper bags in hand, when I saw a short stack of books on a stoop's bottom step only a few brownstones closer to Eighth Avenue than mine. I was obliged to put down my groceries to access the offerings. No need to identify the top two books, something about calculus (a subject I'd never gotten around to in school and probably would've flunked if I had) and a cookbook of indeterminate authorship.

It was the third book that not only caught my eye but dazzled it: *The Great Gatsby,* an edition that I, as a compulsive *Great Gatsby* collector, had been after for years— the 1953 edition, Hal Siegel cover art of a handsome man in the foreground and a twenties roadster in the background. There it was. Right there. In plain sight. I'd say I couldn't believe my eyes, but the gorgeous truth is I could believe my eyes. I was holding it. As of that minute, that moment, it was mine.

Before anyone else could snatch it—how could I be certain another F. Scott Fitzgerald idolator with a *Great Gatsby* jones wasn't skulking nearby?—I put it in one of the grocery bags and headed home, farther west down the street to my apartment and the vaunted *Gatsby* shelves.

Before I carry on further, I need to explain a few personal facts. Anyone picking up this agitated reminiscence might assume by the title that it concerns the couple of deaths—Myrtle Wilson and/or Jay Gatsby himself— that occur in Fitzgerald's long-acclaimed novel. This is assuming whoever is reading this sentence has also read the undisputed twentieth-century classic, which, believe it or don't, is now out of copyright. The 1925 volume is handiwork I consider the only perfect novel I have ever encountered. Saying this as another writer, I wouldn't add a word to *The Great Gatsby* or subtract a word from it, let alone a phrase, sentence or paragraph. My advice is to get hold of it posthaste for a terrific, unforgettable couple hours. But not this minute.

It's my devotion to Fitzgerald's bestseller that got me into the fracas I'm chronicling here, although several other categorizations could just as easily—and perhaps more explicitly and pertinently—apply.

I'm such a *Gatsby* flag-waver that I've made something of a big deal about the book ever since I read it in a prep school English class—Frederick A. Patterson, known to us wiseass preppies as "Fap," being the fastidious teacher and fellow *Gatsby* fanatic.

Since then, I've spent so much more of my hard-earned cash than I'd like to advertise amassing the devastating Fitzgerald collection that I've amassed: two (and counting) wide bookshelves, double-lined with *Gatsby* editions. I do own a signed first edition for which, as you might guess, I paid a pretty penny. Many more than a few pretty pennies. No need to state how many. Too embarrassed. I'm especially embarrassed to say that sitting atop a few of the hardback and paperback editions is a Kindle on which I've downloaded the precious novel. I will say I'm so sold on *TGG* that whenever a new edition is published and I hear about it, I immediately purchase a copy.

Not only to add to the ever-lengthening shelves but to reread what is typically a paperback. I don't just shelve the new acquisition the minute it enters my booklined quarters, I drop everything, sit down in my habitual reading chair with the adjacent standing lamp and end table and crack the new spine. ("Crack" is figurative; I would never actually crack a book's spine.)

My actions are in line with a determination to reread *The Great Gatsby,* new edition or no, at least once a year. Sometimes I reread it twice. There was even one year I reread it three times, the first two back to back. It's not a long read, being well under two hundred pages in all, or most, editions of which I'm aware.

If you're saying to yourself, he must have the confounded thing committed to memory by now, you'd be just about right. I just about do. So much so that I could be one of the characters in Ray Bradbury's *Fahrenheit 451,* who walk around reciting novels due to their being banned in that tome's society. That could be me passionately uttering those final lines: "So we beat on, boats against the current, borne back ceaselessly into the past." (Is any book from literary annals through the ages able to claim a better final sentence? All the alliterative "b"s working their propulsive power.)

My collection runs mostly to paperbacks, as you'd expect, but I don't have them all—with their varying cover art. Needless to say, my owning a first edition indicates that I have the Francis Cugat (otherwise known as

Francisco Coradal-Cougat) image on its cover. (Trivia: He was bandleader Xavier Cugat's brother.) I also have the revered initial image on the 1970 edition when Scribner's decided it was time to revive the evocative painting: a woman's eyes brooding above a metropolitan nightscape. Subsequent editions have also gone back to Cugat, one quite recently.

I even have the Cambridge University Press *Trimalchio* honoring the seventy-fifth anniversary of *The Great Gatsby*'s publication, the version being Fitzgerald's first take on the masterpiece. (Trimalchio, for those who don't know, is a Gatsby-like party-giver introduced in Petronius's *Satyricon*.)

But—and this is the dramatic *but*—it's a very particular later *Great Gatsby* edition that's prompted what you're scanning. You see, there have remained a few editions I lack. Five, I think. (I haven't an accurate counting of all English-language editions; I don't collect foreign editions, Lord have mercy.)

Therefore, it follows that I'm always on the *qui vive* to find them, compulsively rifling through used-bookstore bins and the like. The hours I've devoted to my relentless quest! I never know when and where one will turn up.

Entering my apartment—where rarely a first-time guest has arrived without saying something along the lines of a wide-eyed "What a lot of books!"—I stopped in the kitchen only long enough to refrigerate the foodstuffs that required refrigeration.

Without shedding an overcoat—the April weather was warm; I wasn't wearing an overcoat—I darted directly to my trusty reading chair, turned on the lamp (on the brightest days my living room is on the dark side) and began to read, "In my younger and more vulnerable years..."

That's when it began, not the famed Fitzgerald tale but the reason why I'm writing this, this, this—well, outburst is as good a word as any. So is outcry. So's an Edvard Munch-like scream.

I had barely finished reading the first sentence when a strange thing happened. I'd say the strangest thing happened, if it weren't that even stranger things were to follow.

As my eyes passed over the introductory sentence, the word "vulnerable" began to glow. I caught that in my peripheral vision. At first, I was tempted to ignore it as a trick of optics, but when I looked directly at the "vulnerable," the glow was fading. To confirm that I had it right, I reread the phrase. Lo and behold (I invoke the "lo and behold" deliberately), the "vulnerable" again took on a glow. That wasn't all. This time a spark flew off the page, then a second and third spark whereupon the blasted (I use the adjective deliberately) word popped into italics and then all capital letters. Only for an instant before settling on the page in its—can I say?—proper form.

What was going on? What in literal blazes was going on? Whatever it was had to do with my eyes. I rubbed them and looked at "vulnerable" again. At this latest gawp it only shimmered. Was the lamp throwing an unfamiliar light on the page? I checked the lamp. I hadn't inadvertently shifted it. Nothing there had changed.

I remembered this was early spring and so allergy season. Maybe my annual allergy bout was kicking in, which it usually doesn't until later in April or May. It was early April. I dismissed the possibility as perhaps related to climate change. Or, I thought, could this odd phenomenon mean cataracts? I'm too young to have developed cataracts, I tried to convince myself. On the other hand, I knew that some poor *shlimazels* develop cataracts early.

Deciding I'd make an appointment with my ophthalmologist to be sure, I waved off the episode and continued to read. Resuming my delight in Fitzgerald's prose and narrator Nick Carraway's recollections of his father's sage advice about the inadvisability of criticizing people without first knowing their life's circumstances, I advanced well into the first chapter's second paragraph and was going great guns until I reached this: "...made me the victim of a..."

Whoa. Woe is me. As I skimmed over "victim," again the word took on a glow, fired off a spray of sparks and exploded into itals and all caps, letters also erupting into larger type. Again, I blinked and rubbed my eyes. "Victim" held its new ground but only for another second or two before retreating to its proper size.

"I don't know what's going on," I said—I think out loud—"but I'm not going to pay attention for another second."

Fewer than four or five seconds passed when I swooped into the next sentence and perused "The abnormal mind is quick to detect..." At that, "The abnormal mind" began behaving abnormally and "detect" shimmered and shook.

Rubbing my eyes wasn't likely to do any good, so I didn't bother. I just focused anew on "The abnormal mind" and "detect." The attention paid resulted in such a round of sparks and flares, the sentence could have passed for a Fourth of July fireworks confection.

All right, I decided, something is going on here. But what? Oh, I see, I'm hallucinating. But why? I hadn't been drinking. I'm not much of a drinker. I'm so ignorant about wine that friends mock me: "Daniel, what's the difference between a Neuchatel and a muscatel?"

And this was only a couple minutes past eleven in the morning. I'm not on drugs. Drugs scare me, always have. More than one physician has had to give me a pep talk about following the instructions on a legitimate prescription.

More to the point, I could look around the room and nothing happened out of the ordinary. No hint of double vision. I could focus squarely and reassuringly on my familiar walls, furniture, rugs and, perhaps more fittingly, on my *Great Gatsby* bookshelves.

Okay, but what of the *Gatsbys* (sp?: *Gatsbies*) on the shelves? I got up, went to them, pulled out the first edition, thumbed to the opening page and read. Nothing happened, no glowing, no itals, no cap letters, no sparks, no nothing. I replaced it, picked out another at random, went through the same procedure. Again nothing. I consulted several more. Nothing, nothing, nothing.

The just-acquired Fitzgerald edition, however, which I returned to, had become a carnival of surprises. I looked back at that memorable opening page and read a bit further. Was it equally shocking that words like "secret grief," "wild, unknown men," "hostile," "unmistakable sign," "intimate revelations," "obvious suppression" and the even more insistent string that goes, "I am still a little afraid of missing something" began to carry on like the festivities Doctor Seuss describes in the later pages of *And to Think That I Saw It on Mulberry Street*. Also, and more immediately, like one of Jay Gatsby's West Egg blowouts.

Looking repeatedly at the literally sparkling words for minutes, I finally settled on "I am still a little afraid of missing something." Was I missing something? I went back to the top of the page to re-re-re-reread "victim" and "detect" and the others. The more I did, the more I felt an entirely new sensation. It was as if there was a hand on my left hand guiding it to a succession of words, all of them still dancing to beat the band.

The hand pressed harder, firmer. The grip was determined; I couldn't free myself from it. Was I dreaming? I tried to wake myself, but I could not.

I wasn't dreaming. I was as awake as I could be.

Without easing off, the hand pulled mine to the word "victim" and "detect" and back to "victim" and then "detect" and did this a few more times.

As it did, I realized I'd begun to hear a low moan, a haunting moan that grew in volume. Or was it more like a low sob? Was it Fitzgerald's Daisy Buchanan's sobbing? It was as if I were listening to profound despair rising from...at first, I thought from purgatory. Then it was as if from the grave. Then I thought it came from somewhere much closer. Then the nearly muffled words "Remember me" buzzed in my right ear and echoed. Then they were in my left ear. It was as if I were Hamlet listening to the ghostly importuning of his late father.

I wasn't Hamlet. I remember my late father, Lester

Jules Freund, without his having to remind me. So whom was I to remember? I think I said that aloud as well. If I did or even if I didn't, I again felt the invisible hand pulling mine no longer toward "victim" and "detect" but to the other words that had blared and flared and scintillated before—"secret grief," "wild, unknown men," "hostile," "unmistakable sign," "intimate revelations," "obvious suppression."

Having done that, it forced my hand to the bottom of the page. There, it pushed me to start rapidly flipping across pages. As it did, certain words took on their own glow, threw off sparks, went through the same fiery revelry that emerged on the opening page.

I won't list them all. It's enough that words like "death," "murdered," "got what he deserved," "instantly killed," "mystery," "dead man," "an unpleasantness in the air," "lurking," "morbid," "hearse," "life violently extinguished," "God sees everything," "careless people," "solemn," "helpless," "poor son of a bitch" and "body" got the glow-sparks-itals-all-caps-et-cetera treatment until it reached—and hyperbolized (if there's such a word)—Fitzgerald's poetic last words: "borne back ceaselessly into the past."

Oh, yes, there were also the words "lay a hand on his shoulder."

It was as if I were expected to put the words together and come up with a story, a message of some kind. I remained puzzled, apparently so much so that the hand led me through *The Great Gatsby* 1953 once more. Then the all-but-broadcasting edition closed, and while it lay idle in my lap, I ran the cumulative words and phrases in order and then out of order in my dizzied head—always starting with "victim" and "detect."

Within only a few minutes, I heard myself say to myself, "Dummkopf, don't you get it? I'm telling myself a story."

Not quite right. But close. *The Great Gatsby* is telling me a story, and it's not F. Scott Fitzgerald's. It's not Fitzgerald's story of nice guy Nick Carraway spending three or four months observing arriviste Jay Gatsby's attempt to undo the marriage between those "careless people" Daisy and Tom Buchanan and gal pal Jordan Baker.

I was being told the story of an altogether different occurrence. I was being informed by the disembodied hand that a second tale of malfeasance was embedded in this *Great Gatsby* edition—not, it furthermore appeared, in this edition but in this very copy.

Was it possible that from this very copy, Fitzgerald himself and maybe even Nick Carraway, the Buchanans, Jordan Baker and others were ceasing their explosive intermingling to contact me—"reach out" to me, in the current vernacular—for some cogent reason? Was it Scott Fitzgerald's hand I was feeling?

A man gets killed. There's a death. There's a victim. It's a mystery. The copy and its famous figures want someone to clear up the unpleasantness in the air, to expose something morbid. Someone is needed to detect the facts behind a victim whose life has been violently extinguished, the person who may, or may not, have gotten what he deserved.

Furthermore, somewhere the murderer is lurking, possibly so pleased at getting away with murder that the notion of another murder is playing fast and loose with his or her mind.

How intriguing, I thought as I sat there contemplating the astounding discovery. So splendid a discovery that I replayed it a few times. Imagine that, a copy of a book disclosing a mystery within the mystery of Jay Gatsby, disclosing at least one death for which the careless murderer (murderess?) is never charged.

For more than a few minutes, I delighted in the unexpected revelations. I exulted in them long enough for the delay of my second "Dummkopf, don't you get it?"

And what was it that I still hadn't gotten? This F. Scott Fitzgerald found object wasn't merely telling me a story as if I were another sleepy camper gathered around a fire so that a fun-loving counselor might try to scare me shitless before taps.

A tremor bolted down my spine as I realized I was

being instructed. I was being recruited. It was a tremor enforced by the invisible hand that had steered mine a few minutes earlier.

What hadn't at first been clear to me was suddenly as clear as a Waterford crystal pitcher. I was being informed in no uncertain terms—okay, perhaps in some slightly uncertain terms—that the owner of this *Great Gatsby* copy being disposed of had been murdered, very likely while reading (rereading?) it. Or more's the horror, whoever had owned this very *Great Gatsby* copy was the murderer.

No, that couldn't be. I have always had a good imagination. To my eventual chagrin, I have even boasted about my writer's imagination. But my imagination has never been so good that it could cause words on a printed page to frolic the way these had and then additionally had made something up along such solemn lines.

I reiterated my disbelief for another minute or so when, without warning, the obstinate hand seized mine again and forced it to reopen the *Great Gatsby* copy and led it to page 127. I must not have been privy to 127 before. What does the hand want me to see? No word was coming to bizarre life.

Then I saw it. Halfway down the righthand page in the by-now yellowing margin was a brown smudge. Or was it just a smudge? Was it the color that dried blood assumes when aging on a sepia page? At closer perusal it began to resemble a thumbprint. A bloody thumbprint? At even closer perusal than that, it began a sidestep in the margin that kept up until it swaggered off the page and disappeared.

I couldn't be sure. Still, it came to me: the impression that there had been a murder—an unsolved murder—and therefore a murderer was on the loose. More than that, much more than that, I was designated the person to solve the mystery. If there were another way to interpret the persisting signs, I couldn't discern what it might be.

I gave my indisputable inference another minute's reckoning, and while I did, I again felt the roving hand. This time it pressed three times just over my right shoulder blade, as if it were patting me on the back for a job well done, for a conclusion well drawn and, worse, for a decision bravely reached.

Wait a minute. Did the hand think I was going to do anything about the grim situation to which I just been made privy?

Not by a country mile. Not me. Not this growing boy. Not my cup of herbal tea. Not up my nightmare alley.

The hand again, this time in the middle of my back. And not just a pat. Closer to a wallop. Was this going to keep up as long as I, er, demurred? Would it only desist when I committed to put on my figurative deerstalker hat and get out my figurative magnifying glass? Or even then?

I had a magnifying glass. Perhaps I'd better take my chances. Sure thing, I'll wax and tweak my (nonexistent) mustache, repeat "*tiens, tiens*" and play Hercule Poirot for a week or so, pay some lip service to the unbidden assignment.

Why not? I had some spare time over the next day or two. I'm a writer between novels as well as being between romances. (No call for running my credits here in either category.) When I turn up nothing, I'd have to have earned some points for giving it the old college try. I could then be dismissed as a game, if not successful, sport.

The hand, the Siegel edition itself, would be satisfied. It might even be a nice diversion. I'd always liked reading mysteries and detective fiction though never writing any. Why not live my own? Approach it as good fun, regard it as a hot time in the old town.

The hand again on my back: three pats I took to be appreciative.

I'd start immediately. I wouldn't even finish this *Great Gatsby* reread. The edition was in my possession. I could return to it at any time. And would return to it, you can bet on that and be a winner.

I reran the facts(?). I rechecked the hints I had. Was it Colonel Mustard in the study with the candlestick? That sort of thing. But no, I didn't even have that kind of information.

Yes, I knew—or seemed to know—that in a building near mine a murder had been committed, but I didn't know, now that I'd come to think of it, enough to know whether that benighted townhouse had been the home of the murdered or the home of the murderer.

Before anything else, I'd better figure out which was what, if only to know whether the murderer was still living there. It was likely that snooping around a murderer's home would be a mite more dangerous than sneaking around the digs of the murdered personage.

I firmly righted the weirdly enchanted book on the table and marshaled my feelings. I was anxious. That's one feeling I never have trouble pinpointing. Anxiety could be my middle name. At the same time, I was excited, excitement a feeling I experience far less often than anxiety, which is a mystery for another time.

I glanced at my watch. Since I was raring to go, might I not as well follow the raring and go? But to start when and how? Since stoops are a common amenity on my block of row houses, it seemed like a good idea to sit on mine and keep an eye on the in-question building near me while I made plans for further action. I had the time.

As I'd done my shopping between 10:00 and 11:00, had found my newly acquired Fitzgerald classic shortly after 11:00 and had succumbed to the hand of fate just after 11:30, it was now only a minute or two before noon.

I patted the book on the end table and left my second-floor apartment to sit on the stoop, as brownstone dwellers often do. Nothing unusual about that, unusual for me but not unusual. A neighbor seeing me there wouldn't suspect anything out of the ordinary.

In no more than a minute I was deployed there. It was still a sunny early-April day. As far as anyone could tell, I was just taking the still-early-spring sun and air. I had no reason to assume anyone would suspect that newly self-appointed amateur detective Freund was surveilling.

I looked casually at the townhouse of interest. The books, minus the one I'd claimed, were still there but no longer neatly stacked, as I'd left them. At least one other person must have gone through them.

I slowly swiveled my head as anyone relaxing on a brownstone stoop might do. No reason to arouse suspicions. As luck would have it, not five minutes passed when an athletic-looking young man perhaps in his late twenties with floppy hair and wearing a maroon hoodie, jeans and flipflops appeared, made his way quickly down the neighboring stoop and headed my way, whistling. He was so thin he could have passed for a grandson of Ichabod Crane.

When he reached my stoop, he nodded hello and was about to be continuing on his way. I stopped him. "Excuse me, neighbor," I said. "I wonder if I can ask you a question?"

He stopped, turned back slightly and said, "Sure, if it doesn't take too long. I'm kinda in a hurry."

"Not long at all. I was just wondering about the building you came out of. I guess you live there."

"Yeah," he said pleasantly enough in a high Ichabod Crane twang. "What about it? No vacancies, far as I know."

"That's not it. I've been living on this block a while and from time to time I've heard—I hope you don't mind my saying this—that there was once—I'll be blunt about it—a murder in your building."

"Really? Wow. If there was, I never heard about it, but I've only been living there"—he pointed at the building with a thin Ichabod-Crane index finger—"a while. Maybe that's not the kind of thing you tell prospective renters or buyers."

"I guess not," I said, ready to let it drop.

He was ready to go. "I'd like to know about that myself. You want to ask somebody who's lived there longer. I don't know many of the others. Typical Manhattan, but I have talked to the lady who lives on the second-floor rear. She seems like the kind of busybody every building has at least one of."

"I guess I'm not that interested," I lied. "Thanks anyway."

"Sure thing," he said and walked off. Before he got more than eight or ten feet away, I heard a twanged "Murder! Awesome!" from his direction.

I watched him walk to the far end of the block and turn right. When he was out of sight, I rose with purpose, went over to the building in question and walked up the stoop with purpose. I consulted the directory nailed to the front door right frame.

Apartment 2R was occupied by E. Belfer. I pushed the button. No immediate response. I buzzed a second time. "Who is it? What do you want?" I heard in a scratchy voice through intercom static.

Good question. What did I want? "I wonder if I might speak to you," I said, not knowing what I was going to say next, but as a writer I'm used to making up dialogue. It came to me. "I'm writing a book about unsolved New York City murders and am picking out buildings at random in Manhattan to see what I might turn up." I fleshed out the ad lib. "It seems like a reasonable enough approach. I've already done Staten Island and the Bronx."

"Sounds like a foolish way to go about writing a book," the voice said. "Why don't you just go through police archives?"

She had a point. "I've already done that," I ad-libbed

further. In for a penny, in for a pound. I was talking as fast as I could think. "But you know how cops are. They're touchy about unsolved crimes. Police detectives are glad enough to tell you—at great length—about the ones they closed the book on. But unsolved murders? Zipped lips. I've been forced to go about my research in this way."

"Yessiree," the voice said. (I didn't know there were people who still said "yessiree.") "I've had the zipped-lip treatment from cops, too," the scratchy voice went on. I bet she had. I was getting the picture of a woman who didn't restrict busybodying to her immediate premises. "I'll come down to talk to you. I don't let strangers in just like that. A' course, I don't know what I can tell you. Just wait on the stoop a minute. What's your name anyway? I'm Estelle Belfer. That's Ms. Estelle Belfer."

What name should I give her? I decided I might as well give her my real name. I said, truthfully, "Daniel Freund."

"Just wait there on the stoop, Daniel Freund," I heard, the voice already fading. "I'll be right down."

Ms. Belfer, in, I'd say, her early seventies, emerged quickly enough. She was—still is—a short, stocky woman with a busy face not unlike the side of a walnut shell. She was wrapped in a man's flannel bathrobe whose better days might have been in the nineteen-thirties or forties. She held the outer door open and asked, "You're Mr. Freund?"

"Yes."

"Like I said, there's nothing I can tell you, but I didn't want to be rude. The book you say you're writing sounds interesting, but there was never any murder here."

"Are you sure?" I asked. "A few people on this block told me there might be."

"I don't know who they are and where they got that. I've only been living here for forty-three years, and I never heard it. I would've, don't you think?"

I sensed I wasn't going to get anything more from the adamant Ms. Belfer. I couldn't very well tell her a copy of *The Great Gatsby* discarded on her stoop wised me up that there'd been a murder right under her nose or, at the very least, a murderer. I said, "I'm sorry to have disturbed you, Ms. Belfer. I must have misunderstood what I was told."

I started to leave when Ms. Belfer said, "Before you go, you might want to help yourself to one or two of those books down there. I put them there myself. They're not mine, though. They belonged to a man who committed suicide a few years back. Oh, yes, we did have a suicide. He stored them in boxes and more in the basement. They've been sitting there since then. I figured I might as well get rid of them after all this time. He isn't going to miss them."

I pretended to do her bidding. Holding the book on

calculus and the cookbook I had ignored before, I put them on one of the trash cans next to the stoop and said, as off-handedly as I knew how, "You say there was a man who committed suicide?"

"It was quite something," Ms. Belfer said and then, "Could you put those books on the stoop with the others? I don't like anything sitting on the trash cans." Keeping a tight grip on the bathrobe, while standing against the door so it wouldn't close behind her, Ms. Belfer waxed confidential. She repeated, "Oh yes, it was quite something. This man Fulton Cutler took his life some years ago now, maybe even as long as three years, maybe a little more. I'm not too good on dates. That's as long ago as his apartment has stayed unsold. Still on the market, still furnished."

She pointed toward a sign attached to a wall by the door. How had I missed it? Didn't speak well for my prospective detective acumen. It said, "For Sale. Reasonably Priced Floor-Through Apartment. Contact: Harold Swirner, Swirner & Swirner, swirnerandswirnerrealtors .com" with a phone number I quickly memorized. I have a good memory for phone numbers. It's a Freund-family knack that comes in handy more than you might think.

Ms. Belfer was saying, "Once prospective buyers learn what awful thing happened in that apartment, they don't want it. I've had to inform a few of them myself. Maybe the word got around anyway. Swirner doesn't show the place that often." I could already tell I'd do well to believe her. "I wouldn't want to move into an apartment where someone shot himself. Would you? It's bad enough I have to live over it."

She was waiting for my response, but I had other questions. "A suicide, you say, Ms. Belfer?"

"Oh yes." She held on to the "oh" much longer this time. "Took his life, he did. Quite a thing at the time."

"And they were convinced it was a suicide? Not a murder?"

"It couldn't have been a murder. Fulton Cutler had to have shot himself. Mr. Fulton Cutler, if you please. What kind of name is Fulton, anyway? Showing off family wealth, if you ask me. Or trying to. He was slumped at his desk in his rear office. He had the floor-through, you know. The parlor floor, they call it. Hoity-toity. His right arm has hanging down. The gun had fallen out of his hand. With his fingerprints on it."

I was waiting for her to define it as an open-and-shut case.

"I don't like to speak ill of the dead," she continued, "but I was never very fond of Fulton Cutler." I had the distinct impression that she was quite happy to speak ill of the dead. A twinkle in her eye told me so. "He was a strange bird. I tried I don't know how many times to engage him in neighborly conversation. He just wasn't friendly. You know the type. Think they're better than you and me. I finally gave up. I have reason to believe the other tenants, renters and owners alike had the same attitude toward him I did. This is a non-evict co-op, you know, not that I completely understand the ins and outs. I suppose you do."

I did and do, but that's yet another mystery for another time.

Ms. Belfer plunged back into her disquisition. "Then when he shot himself, I said to myself, 'That figures.' Not that I didn't feel sorry for him."

"But it was a suicide. You're certain of that?"

"An open-and-shut case." She said it. "Had to be. The door to the study was locked from inside. The police verified that. How they got the door unlocked I'm pretty sure I know. They got a locksmith. A small van saying locksmith pulled up here the afternoon they found him. Well, they didn't find him. The housekeeper, who came every Monday, Wednesday and Friday—Ms. Bishop, a nice woman; I liked her—didn't really find him, but she thought something was up. He never locked that door, she said. So she called the cops. It's a good thing, too. Once they got in, they saw the windows were secure. There was no other way in or out.

"I learned all that from the detectives who were

coming and going for days. I kept running into them. By accident. Once Mr. Fulton Cutler was discovered, I told them everything I knew, which wasn't much more than I just told you." She took a pause. Was it for dramatic effect? If so, she got it when she said, "Then there was the suicide note."

Again, I employed an offhand tone. "A suicide note?" I wasn't about to make this a dramatic-effects contest.

"Oh yes." She exaggerated the "oh" again but even more so. "The cops in and out of here—and the coroner and funeral people—for those couple of days wouldn't say anything about it, but I wasn't deterred." She loaded extra oomph into "deterred."

"I'm sure you weren't, Ms. Belfer. Do go on."

"I was about to. I often happened to be on the stoop as they were parading around, and the day after the suicide, one of the cops—I don't think she was a detective; I don't remember—was coming out with several items in plastic bags and let one of them fall. Right where I was standing. 'I think you dropped something,' I said to her. But not before I picked it up and had a good look at it."

"I bet you did, Ms. Belfer." I was having some fun with her, but she was too immersed in her reportage to notice. I'd already pegged her as a woman who noticed what she wanted to notice and did not notice what she deemed not worth noticing.

"Of course, I looked at it. Tenants should watch over their buildings, don't you agree?" I nodded assent. "Not everybody understands that obligation. A number of them live right here in this very building."

"You were saying about the dropped plastic bag."

"It was a single piece of fancy paper, you know, the kind of expensive stationery hifalutin people have. His name was at the top—Fulton Cutler in fancy-shmancy letters. Embossed, I think is what they call it. It said—I memorized it—'I've had enough of this.' Just that. 'I've had enough of this.' He'd had enough! We've all had enough, but we don't go around bumping ourselves off, do we?"

An answer was required. "No, we don't," I said, which satisfied her. To say Ms. Belfer was enjoying her confidences is an understatement, but that wasn't my primary takeaway.

What was was my coming smack up against a locked-room mystery—and on my first amateur-detective go. What a stroke of beginner's luck. For I was certain that's what this fine howdy-do had to be. My *Great Gatsby* copy told me there was a murder attached to its previous owner, and it was now backed up by my years of reading—and watching crime carried out on movie screens and television.

Maj Sjôwall and Per Wahlöö even dubbed one of their mysteries *The Locked Room.*

There was no way around it. I'd hit pay dirt. In fiction I'd never seen a locked-room situation immediately labeled a suicide by thick-headed chief police detectives that wasn't proved within days to be a murder, by either Philo Vance himself or the legion of Philo Vance acolytes.

It had to be.

Ms. Belfer wasn't finished. (Was she ever finished, I wondered?) She said, leaning out from the door and once again in *sotto voce* confidence, "I always thought there was something fishy about the whole thing. Fulton Cutler was an oddball character. Nothing I could put my finger on, mind you."

"But you had your misgivings. Very interesting," I said.

Ms. Belfer smiled an abashed smile in recognition of being understood on her surely, as she judged it, nonpareil neighborly New York City manners. "Thank you," she said, "not everyone has your insight."

"And thank you, Ms. Belfer, but I fear I've taken up too much of your valuable time."

"Not at all, Mr. Freund. I always try to make time in my busy day to talk to agreeable strangers. I wish you luck on your search." That said, she bowed slightly in my direction and backed through the door toward, I expected, her second-floor home, the one directly above the former Fulton Cutler's.

I stood where I was—by the trash cans—for a second to decide my next move. It seemed obvious, didn't it? I had to get into that previously locked room. But on what pretext? How does the average citizen gain access to a previously locked room, a previously locked room in a floor-through apartment currently on the market?

The ever-present, though forever invisible, bulb clicked on over my head. The private dick goes in as a prospective buyer.

With Harold Swirner's telephone number firmly filed away, I hurried home. Ms. Belfer was also on my mind, however. Since she evidently keeps vigil as often as she does, why wouldn't she have long since noticed someone like me entering or exiting my neighboring townhouse? Maybe as I occupied an apartment in the building to the west of hers, she never looked in my direction when she was leaving her building to go east toward the Eighth Avenue shops. Maybe she habitually looked east toward Eighth Avenue as the more promising thoroughfare. Oh, well, she hadn't shown any sign of recognition, more's my good fortune.

In the house, I grabbed my landline. I've kept an often-ridiculed landline for sentimental reasons as much as any other. I dialed Harold Swirner. When a receptionist put me through to him, I wasted no time getting to the point. I said I'd been passing the Twentieth Street

address, saw the sign for a floor-through and was immediately interested, my having searched so long for something that looked and sounded promising. To ladle it on a
little thicker, I said I was getting to be just a bit desperate
to end my quest.

He said that the specified brownstone sounded, without his having met me yet, as if it would be ideal. He
added, lowering his voice conspiratorially, that he could
tell me the apartment had been on the market for some
time and that since this was an estate sale, the executors
were showing signs of being even more desperate to get
rid of it than I was to buy it. "In this case, definitely a
buyer's market," he said in what I recognized as a real
estate broker's well-rehearsed honest-as-the-day-is-long
delivery.

We made an appointment to view the apartment the
following morning at 10:00. Since I was free the rest of
the day, I thought I'd return to going about my other
business, but I had no other business. I have said I am
between engagements but not yet strapped.

One thing I knew I wasn't about to do was return to
reading my latest *TGG* acquisition. I'd had my fill of fireworks displays. I'd gotten the message. Nevertheless, I
had started this unexpectedly-thrust-on-me endeavor
and might as well spend as much of the afternoon as it
takes to finish the reread. So I went to the appropriate

shelves and decided on the signed first edition. For obvious reasons, I considered it the first among equals.

I extracted it from its companions, went to my reading chair, sat down, turned on the reading lamp and dug in. As no words—as none had when I consulted it earlier—glowed or did anything but sit calmly, I was prepared for the remarkable chain of Fitzgerald's tragic events. I could read without fear of interruption.

Yet I had barely finished the opening page when my mind began to wander from Nick Carraway's West Egg. The tale-telling was so poetically inspiring that I again began to think I must have been hallucinating over the 1953 edition.

The thought lasted only a split second. I had already taken that into consideration and had been talked into rejecting it by the book itself. Foolish to spend any more time entertaining the gratuitous notion.

My next quandary was whether I was leaning too far over my skis by appointing myself the detective in this closed suicide case. I was never much of a skier in the first place. But if not me, who? I could go to the police. There was and still is a precinct in the next block east of me. It had to be a good bet they knew about the supposed suicide, had records. Probably case-closed records, whereas I now knew it indisputably was an unsolved cold case.

The only thing to do then was picture myself marching into the precinct and telling the first police officer I saw that my appearance involved a local suicide of some three years past I had reason to believe wasn't a suicide but a murder.

Say he or she even allowed me to speak to the desk sergeant, who would undoubtedly ask what evidence I had to substantiate my claim. I blithely say I have no hard evidence but that a discarded copy of *The Great Gatsby* alerted me. The only circumstance under which anyone would continue to listen would be wanting to humor me long enough for other cops to contact the folks with the straitjackets.

Maybe I was convinced I wasn't hallucinating, but five'll get you ten they wouldn't be.

This was up to me, all right.

No, it wasn't up to me alone. That insight was made manifest from the end table. All the while I was going over this in my mind, I was only somewhat aware of an odd humming. Making myself fully aware of it, I realized the humming locus was the supine *Great Gatsby* 1953. It was informing me we were in this together.

That's crazy, I said to myself. At the word "crazy" the humming stopped. It was replaced by series of quick feminine-like tsk-tsks. Daisy Buchanan again?

I knew enough to say I didn't mean to say "crazy."

Humming resumed.

The rest of the day I gave over to rethinking everything that had happened since the long-desired 1953 edition entered a never-ending collection that would go on to include the many more editions cropping up now that Fitzgerald's copyright had expired and, thanks to public domain, myriad *Great Gatsby* editions would drop thudlike on the market.

TUESDAY

After a nearly sleepless night, I hustled to the compromised address at 10:00 on the dot, preceding fringe-pated Harold Swirner by no more than a minute. He advanced toward me with a determined real-estate-broker smile on his face and keys in his right hand.

My only concern was the possible (probable?) appearance of Ms. Belfer. What good would she be as the in-house busybody if she weren't at her post?

It may have been that Harold Swirner had the same concern. He barely had time to shake my hand when he hurried up the stoop to open the outer door. "You'll love this apartment," he tossed over his shoulder as he opened the inner door. "The only setback it has is nothing to do with the space itself. There's a woman who—how shall I put this?—watches over the building out of the goodness of her heart. That could be her now."

He was responding to the sound of footsteps on the staircase and a raspily dulcet "Hello, hello? Can I help you?"

Harold Swirner already had the key in the lock to the former Fulton Cutler front door. He opened it in a jiffy and not so much beckoned me in as thrust me.

Since Cutler had vacated the place under whatever circumstance, it looked as if nothing had been changed. Strange, I thought, but perhaps the realtors wanted it to look as livable as possible.

The professionally affable Swirner anticipated my observation. "You'll notice the apartment remains nearly as it was. The previous tenant was Fulton Cutler, a man of great taste."

"Yes, I see that," I said.

"When Swirner and Swirner decided to stage the apartment,"—Mr. Swirner put the "stage" in air quotes—"which, you know, you have to do these days, we decided to keep things very much as they were, which you might appreciate. You also look to be a man of taste." Even for a real estate agent, he was piling it on. "As you can see, this is the living room."

He continued down a narrow hall lined with framed music scores. Off it was a small kitchen—"perfectly adequate, if not exactly eat-in, but notice the commodious cabinets and appliances. New oven, I ought to point out," Swirner said, as he hurried along. "The bedroom, and here is the bathroom, also commodious. The marble sink. Handsome, you'll agree."

I muttered and nodded approval.

"And finally, the back room, facing south and allowing much sun to enter through the two windows. The former tenant used this room, as you can see, as a study, but it could be used as a master bedroom."

I entered the sanctum.

It looked exactly as I expected it would. The forest-green walls were booklined. The windows had floor-length maroon curtains edged with gold trim hanging from gilt bars. Two wing chairs upholstered in maroon velvet faced the desk and rested on, I estimated, an eight-by-nine Persian rug featuring birds sitting atop lidded urns. A large landscape painting depicting low hills and a winding river at sunset hung between the windows. It was signed John Frederick Kensett. Hudson River School, I guessed, but could have been wrong. What I know about the history of art can be dodgy. A bronze lighting fixture of masculine heft hung about one foot from the forest-green ceiling. Sconces holding candles that had never been lit rested on the east and west sides of the room.

Just the right aesthetic number of feet from the south wall was a wide wooden desk, behind it an inviting tufted-leather chair pulled back at an angle suggesting it hadn't been moved since Fulton Cutler's corpse had been lifted from it, although it must have been. A study lamp with a green metal shade sat on the desk just above a leather desk blotter. A closed shiny green scrapbook—the word "Scrapbook" in flowery purple gilded letters—also sat on the blotter and by it an open bottle of Flex Seal—no lid—that, when I looked closely, had completely solidified. A heavy pair of brass scissors was on the other side of the scrapbook. There was an open and folded copy of the *New York Times* placed just so. I wasn't going to take the time to see the date on it. What would have been the point, I ask myself in hindsight? None, now that I know what I know.

I took the rest of the room in hurriedly. I hadn't decided whether I would show great interest in it or, in contrast, let Harold Swirner think I wasn't evidencing much interest at all.

"Another attractive room, wouldn't you say?" Harold Swirner ventured but this time without allowing extreme enthusiasm.

"Yes," I said, without giving too much away. I wanted to examine the room for reasons I wasn't going to explain to him. "I'm just thinking about what I might do with a room like this." I was giving it the careful onceover, as if to explore it for my inclinations. "I likely wouldn't keep it the way it is. I guess I should ask whether the furnishings come with the apartment."

"If you're looking for someplace already furnished, that would be something any buyer would have to work out with the estate."

"I'm not, really," I said, my "not really" being a jab at

not appearing to be Harold Swirner's idea of a prospective buyer.

I did continue strolling, as nonchalantly as I could affect, around the room. Since this might likely be my only chance to scope out the room, I was taking as thorough a mental inventory of the items on the desk as I was able. I gazed at the ceiling, gandered the painting. The room was no more than faintly musty. I didn't need to wonder who kept up the apartment—Swirner & Swirner, maybe, with Fulton Cutler estate participation. There was the impression that at least a certain amount of dusting and vacuuming had been done but that the room might well look as it had when Fulton Cutler occupied it—even at his, to me, non-suicidal death.

I went to the room's heavy wooden door and tried it. "I see," I said, "that this door can be locked."

"Only from this side," Mr. Swirner informed me.

I bent over to look more closely at the lock. "I don't see the key. Not that it matters."

"It's a funny thing," Harold Swirner said with a little chuckle, "but the key got lost somehow, misplaced. Not a problem. A locksmith can always replace the lock or adjust it to be locked from both sides."

"But this looks like an antique lock. Could that be done, do you think?"

"If you're not—if a prospective buyer isn't going to

keep the room like this—what's the difference?"

"True enough. I wonder if the, uh, previous owner ever locked it. Why would he if he were the only one in the house?"

"I couldn't say," Harold Swirner said. "Any number of reasons, I guess."

"I suppose you're right. On any number of occasions." I thought about making a joke about locked-room mysteries but held my tongue.

I wandered to the windows and was casually looking out the eastern one. I ought to say I was looking out as casually as I could. "Nice garden," I said.

"The ground-level tenants have the only access to it," Harold Swirner said and broke into broker-ese. "They are responsible for its upkeep. You, if you buy the place, would have the view but not the worries."

"That's to the plus side," I said. "I don't have a green thumb."

I was being offhand so's I could inventory the garden, which was a drop of, say, nine feet, if that. It was coming into spring bloom. A flower bed directly below the windows was divided into two parts by what must be a back door into the ground-floor apartment. Daffodils flourished. There was a large oak tree about two-thirds of the way toward the garden's southern wall. It, too, was beginning to bloom but not yet in full leaf, just leaflets of celadon green. The tree must have been there long before the house was built, it was that old and spreading its branches wide. I noticed a couple of branches had been cut off, perhaps because they'd reached too closely to the building and the windows. At the garden's bottom end a metal ladder leaned against the back wall. A tarpaulin on the small expanse of concrete covered what I took to be garden furniture.

Surveying the contents, as if in full ownership of the primaveral space, was a bulldog. His liveliness may have been nothing more than a need to find the ideal spot to do his business.

Other than giving the dog the run of the airy place, the current occupant or occupants must not yet have spent much time welcoming spring to their little island in the city. I wondered who they were and whether Ms. Belfer might know. I'd bet she would.

As the omnipresent vision of Ms. Belfer came to me, I further thought that as a group, busybodies may be an irritant, but for the amateur detective they could prove to be helpful, maybe even suspects.

I'd hold on to the thought.

I looked out the window a little longer and had the impulse to open it. I tried to raise it by way of the two indented handles at the frame's bottom. I gave a little chuckle and said, "I thought I'd get a better look at the nice view you just praised. I'm afraid not. The window doesn't give. Maybe the other—." I started toward the second window.

"You won't be able to lift that one, either," Mr. Swirner said. "Both windows need an adjustment that hasn't been gotten around to. You know how those things go."

When he said that, I had a minuscule inspiration. Perhaps I ought not to have acted on it, but my copious urges can get the better of me. I said, "What with the jammed windows and the lock on the study door, you could say that were the door locked, the occupant would be in a locked room." I lightened the remark by adding, "That might be a preferable situation for someone who enjoys absolute solitude. So many people do, more men, I venture to say, than women."

Having made the small observation, I again kept myself from saying anything about the popularity of locked-room deaths in detective fiction.

"Yes, men do just that," he said, set on changing the subject. "Way-yull, that's about the length and breadth of the tour. Is there anything else I can show you? Or any questions you might have?"

"The apartment sure is nice," I said. "Makes me wonder why it's been on the market as long as you say. Or did you say?"

Mr. Swirner held his professional smile in place. "I

don't know if I did or didn't. It's been a couple years, long enough for the executors to get nervous. You just never can tell about these things. I've seen some places that can't hold a candle to this one fly off the market in a matter of days and others I regard as much more saleable not even get an insulting low bid for months, years even. Like I said on the phone, it's a buyer's market." He waved both arms at the surroundings, then turned his palms downward in a good-riddance-to-bad-rubbish gesture. "By now, the Cutler estate just wants to get it off their hands."

As he and I headed to the apartment door and out into the hallway, Harold Swirner locked the door behind us. We proceeded through the double-door entrance, Mr. Swirner leading the way, looking furtively around. It didn't take much of a guess on my part that he was checking the narrow horizon for Ms. Belfer.

"Yes," I said as if I were taking in nothing but was conscientiously sizing up what we'd just seen. "I like the apartment. I'll be giving it some serious thought. I'm not certain it's exactly what I'm looking for, but it does come close."

"Remember it's a buyer's market," Mr. Swirner said while still scouting for Ms. Belfer. As we reached the first of the entrance doors, he located her. She was standing outside at the top of the stoop.

Guiding me through that door and then the outer door, Harold Swirner said, "You must forgive me, Mr.

Freund, I've just realized I'm late for my next appointment. I have to run."

As we cleared the outer door but not Ms. Belfer, Mr. Swirner tightened his grip on my arm. "Hello there, Ms. Belfer," he said, somewhat short of breath. "I hope you're well." He was hurrying me down the steps.

That's when Ms. Belfer said cheerily to me, "I know you. Weren't you just here yesterday asking about—?"

I knew what she was leading up to and cut her off. "Yes, I was, Ms. Belfer. I'm the one asking about the floor-through apartment for sale." Mr. Swirner still held my arm vise-like, but now I was the one hastening him away from the scene of the unsolved crime and the irrepressible stoop vigilante. "And you were an enormous help. You can see I was just looking at it."

Behind me I heard "But-but-but-but," as if Ms. Belfer was mimicking a motorboat with a recalcitrant engine.

Ignoring that, I said to Mr. Swirner, "When I passed the building yesterday, Ms. Belfer—that is her name, isn't it?—introduced herself and filled me in on the building."

"She did, did she?" he said with a lean and hungry look. "How much—uh, what did she tell you?"

"Not that much, really. Some of what you told me. About the apartment being on the market for a while. What kind of building it is. Quiet. Something about the previous occupant."

"Nothing more?"

I took pity on Harold Swirner. To put him at his ease and off my tail I said, "I didn't have to hear any more. I pegged her pretty quickly as one of those people who butt into everybody's business."

"Sounds like you got her in one," Mr. Swirner said. The look of relief he let go wouldn't have been out of place in a Tylenol commercial.

We reached the southwest corner at Eighth Avenue. Harold Swirner had let go of my arm several feet back and said, "I need to be on my way, as I mentioned. You'll let me know what you think." In one sweeping motion, he pulled his card out of a jacket pocket, handed it to me and hailed a passing cab. Leaping for it, he swung back and said, "Where are my manners? Can I drop you anywhere?"

"Thanks, but no," I said. "I'm going to look around the neighborhood a bit." I meant to imply that the neighborhood was unfamiliar to me, but I didn't want to be explicit. I'd be lying. As if I hadn't been dissembling like the devil for the last half-hour, for the last day.

I wanted, instead of scoping out an area I knew quite well, to go home and think about what I'd just explored but, I told myself, had explored insufficiently.

Sitting minutes later in my trusty reading chair and holding a pad and pencil—is this the way detectives work?—I started thinking about practiced detectives Holmes, Wimsey, Maigret, Nero Wolfe in their favored chairs. I concentrated on the formerly lockable, presently unlocked room.

Before I forgot what I'd tallied in my mind, I jotted down everything I could remember of Fulton Cutler's study. The list was long. What struck me wasn't the items, the accessories, the furnishings that I recalled but the notion—would a proper detective call it a hunch?—that there were things I'd seen that raised questions I had yet to ask myself.

What were they? Where were they? I pictured the room as a whole, as if panning its three-hundred-sixty degrees. I homed in on areas. I zeroed in on the desk. Something about the desk. Something about the desk. Was it one of the items there or something not there that should have been? Not the "suicide note." Something else. Not the scrapbook. Not the scissors. Not the Flex Seal. Or was it the Flex Seal? Something about the Flex Seal stuck in my mind like a splinter in a thumb. I don't know, but it was something. I tracked in on the windows with their decorator's draperies. Not helpful. Not helpful enough.

Was it my imagination, or was it a satisfied hum I heard coming from the direction of the newly acquired *Great Gatsby?* It was the increasingly familiar hum.

I'd done my best relying on my memory while at the

scene of the presumed crime—not that suicide isn't a crime—but I now knew I needed to get back there, and pronto.

But how?

The obvious gatekeeper was real estate agent Swirner. I was reluctant. I didn't want to string him along to the point where he was on to me. Were I to have him show me the premises again, I would likely not be able to take the time I might need for the inklings I had to click into place. Truth to tell, there was no need for me to contact Harold Swirner, much less see him ever again.

Which I never did.

How about a super? I'd never given that any thought. Perhaps that might pan out. But what were the reasons I could give a super for the kind of survey I was contemplating?

The only other approachable open-sesame was Ms. Belfer. I had no reason to believe she had a key to the former Fulton Cutler digs, but she had convinced me—and Harold Swirner—that she knew more about the building she either had not yet gotten around to spilling or hadn't yet thought of probing. More than that, she unquestionably seemed to have (unwitting?) accomplice potential.

In addition, Ms. Belfer was the handiest, but just how honest about my motives—no, "honest" may not mean what I want to say—did I want to be? I wasn't certain. If

I wasn't certain, then I had better hold off on the nature of my interest.

I'd met Harold Swirner at 10:00. It was now getting close to 1:00. I'd try to catch Ms. Belfer in her customary outpost. Out I went, but carefully. I didn't want her to see me coming from my building. I pushed ajar my outer door, looked through its glass pane. There was Ms. Belfer, talking to the postman—our proficient Calvin of the troublesome knees—who was standing to the left of Ms. Belfer and causing her to be angling away from my vantage point.

I hurried down my stoop toward hers, watching hers just as Calvin was resuming his trek. "Oh, hello, Ms. Belfer."

"I thought I saw you leaving here a while ago," she inserted, wasting no time to get to the bottom of my visit.

"I know. I must apologize for not stopping to say hello. Mr. Swirner was in a hurry to get somewhere else."

"Oh, was he?" What Ms. Belfer could wring from an "oh" was truly impressive. "He's always in a hurry to get somewhere else. That's what you think. That's what he thinks. What he's in a hurry about is not to tell prospective buyers everything there is to know about the Fulton Cutler secret. But you already know it. So, what, if you don't mind me asking, were you doing with him?"

Ms. Belfer caught herself being bluntly inquisitive.

When she got to the "if you don't mind me asking," she softened her voice to the all-but-kittenish.

I was ready for the query. I replied in kind, attaching another (social?) fib. "I really have you to thank for that. If you hadn't talked to me for the few minutes you did yesterday, I might have missed the Swirner and Swirner sign. There was no reason for me to tell you this, but besides searching for buildings where unsolved murders have taken place, I am looking for a new apartment. This one sounded as if it had—has—potential."

(How many outright means-justifying-ends fibs are a detective's prerogative—even the newly self-appointed version?)

Ms. Belfer altered her all-but-kittenish aspect. "You're interested in the apartment? Even though you know the previous owner took his own life?"

"Yes, but I'm not interested despite the supposed suicide attempt," I said, thinking that adding air italics to "despite" would be a nice touch. "I'm interested because of the supposed suicide attempt"—air itals on the "because," too.

It further boosted her attention. "What? You mean you're not the superstitious type?"

"Only about some things," I said, enjoying the opening to nudge her along. "The ordinary ones, you know, like Friday the thirteenth and cracked mirrors. I'm interested despite something else entirely."

This time I relaxed the itals, but I was getting her going. "What's that?" She almost leapt at me. Not kittenish-like. Cat-like. "You want an apartment where there was a suicide? That's what you want? Are you nuts?"

"You see, Ms. Belfer, I don't think Fulton Cutler was a suicide." She mustered another of her but-but-buts. I was quick to put her out of her incipient misery. "You see, I don't think it was a suicide at all. I think it was a murder."

More but-but-buts, mounting in intensity. I chalked it up to the busybody's belief that he, or in this instance she, has the last word on the lowdown.

With emphasis, I said, "Oh, yes, Ms. Belfer, it was a murder, all right."

"But-but-but," she interjected. I decided to let her finish. "The locked room, the gun, the suicide note, the-the-the—." She'd winded herself but not for long. "Isn't it even worse to buy an apartment where there's been a murder? If that's what you think it was. No matter how wrong you are?"

"I grant you, the evidence is there for a suicide," I said, noting her expression lightening, "but it's all circumstantial."

"Convincingly circumstantial, I'd say."

"No question it immediately impresses you—I'm using the general 'you'—that it's convincingly circumstantial, but on closer examination it's a lot less so. Let me ask you this, Ms. Belfer. Were you ever able to examine the room where Fulton Cutler was shot?"

There was a pause so pregnant it almost went into labor. "Well, the detectives on the case did everything they could to keep me out. There were any number of them at the time. I understood why they wouldn't want just anyone to be prying into their investigation, but I'm not just anyone. I know plenty about this building, who comes in and who goes out, all that kind of information. But that cut no ice with them. No, not with them."

"There you are, Ms. Belfer. If you'd gone into the room, I bet you would have your suspicions."

"I might have," Ms. Belfer said, dramatically changing her attitude. A devilish look shot into her suspicious eyes. "I always said I thought there was something fishy about it. I think I said as much to you. The detectives were too closed-lipped. Especially one I didn't like at all. Not a bit." She gave whoever that one was a split-second thought, then picked up where she'd left off. "I did get to thinking they were holding something back. But I have my ways."

"There you go, Ms. Belfer. I mean it when I say that if you'd gone into that room after it had been unlocked, you might have had the same queries I have."

Ms. Belfer had taken on a pleased look, not just pleased with herself but loving the opportunity to be pleased. Pleased that she had indeed been in the room? I wasn't ready to rule that blaring possibility out.

"And I was in the room," I said, snatching the chance to be pleased with myself and knowing I was on the verge of getting what I'd been plotting. "I have spotted the elusive clues you yourself might have spotted."

Yup, I fed her the line to see if by any chance she, newshound that she was, had actually noticed something meaningful. I watched her face for a giveaway expression. There was none.

I went on. "In addition to that, I have sensed the absence of clues that were there that hadn't yet been picked up on."

"Maybe," Ms. Belfer said.

"That's just what I was thinking," I said, intending to be devious, and succeeding. "Of course, you have no way to gain entry." That supposedly conversation-stopper comment made, I had more than one Bicycle brand card up my sleeve. "But I bet you know the super, and the super has keys."

"We're between supers. Joey Martino died a couple of months ago. He lived a few doors down and was always on hand." She pointed several doors past my building. "The building owners haven't replaced him yet. Until then, we have to get in touch with them if anything goes wrong. They send someone."

I ran through that information to figure out if there were any alternative openings. Other than Harold Swirner, now off my contact list, who might have keys to Fulton Cutler's crime scene? If I hit on someone, how would I explain my need to revisit the apartment? Who could I purport to be?

Maybe Sam Spade would come up with something. I wasn't yet enough of a flatfoot to accomplish as much. I might never be, this despite my actual flat feet.

So far, I only had enterprising Ms. Belfer on the line. "Gee," I said, "I hate to give up, but I don't want to make a bid on the apartment until I see it again. And—I think you'll understand this—I'm leaving out Harold Swirner. He'd assume I'm genuinely interested and might lean on Fulton Cutler's estate to stick more closely to their asking price."

"You can't do that," Ms. Belfer leapt in. "I wouldn't trust that Harold Swirner as far as I could throw him. And you saw his size. And mine." I knew what I was doing, didn't I? Even more so when she resumed the kittenish guise. "There's always Joey Martino's wife. The widow Martino."

"Why do you bring her up?" I asked with the kind of speed that wins derbies.

"Because she has keys." This announced with a triumphant grin crunching her walnut face.

"She has keys?" I asked. "How do you know that?"

"I borrowed them. I locked myself out of my apartment some time ago and had the presence of mind to think she still might have Joey's keys. She did."

"The estate didn't take them back when Joey died? Or Swirner and Swirner?"

"Sure they did, but she held onto one big ring of keys, in case she wanted to go into the building and find any tools or other things Joey might have left behind. So you can get Joey's keys from her. Or I can."

This was great news. Still, I didn't want to be too enthusiastic about it. "Perhaps," I said, lingering on the "perhaps," "you or I or we could go get them."

I started to walk in the direction she had pointed a few minutes earlier.

"Or," Ms. Belfer said, "we can just use mine."

"Yours?" What kind of cat-and-mouse game were we playing?

"Mine. I'm no fool. When I borrowed Joey's, I had them duplicated in case I locked myself out again. I'd have a second set of keys always on me." She patted a pocket on that day's flannel garment, not a bathrobe but the same vintage. There was the unmistakable jangle of keys. "I thought, if I duplicate the keys to my apartment, why not duplicate all the keys? You never know when they might come in handy. I'd be doing the other tenants a favor."

"Doing the other tenants a favor." Some operator she was. Who was playing whom here? It was as if Doctor Watson had taken charge of the latest case. Or if this were movie casting, Thelma Ritter.

As if to emphasize that, Ms. Belfer pulled the keys from the pocket and shook them. "Shall we?"

"We shall," I nodded, and Ms. Belfer—now my confederate, if not my accomplice—opened the outer and inner doors as well as the door to Fulton Cutler's long-vacated apartment.

"Wait just a second, Ms. Belfer," I said, a thought hitting me like a dart, "if you have the keys to the Cutler apartment, why haven't you used them before now?"

Ms. Belfer drew her flannel shmatte—and herself—up. "Are you suggesting I'm a snoop?"

"Of course not, Ms. Belfer."

"That's better," she said, waving me into the apartment and leaving me in the cold as to whether she'd ever done some lone prying herself. I could only guess. In the affirmative.

We proceeded through the rooms, with which I was now somewhat familiar, to the study, where nothing had been changed. Why would it have been?

I started inspecting the room much more closely than I had when Mr. Swirner was eyeing me. The desk was my first objective. Ms. Belfer had already gotten there.

She was pointing at the several now familiar items as if to count them. Then she did something that startled me. She moved the open Flex Seal a fraction of an inch.

Was she positioning it where she'd previously seen it, if, indeed, she had previously seen it? My money was on a previous sighting. "What are you doing?" I asked, thinking about the Flex Seal can again. Was it that it was too outsized for the other, uh, classier items on the desktop?

"Nothing, I'm not doing anything," she said, "just adjusting the can. I think it looks better this way."

"You shouldn't be rearranging anything. Everything should be left just as it was."

"Oh, no," she said, throwing me a squint I understood was meant to be a wink. "It's all been changed from whatever it was. The police detectives took care of that. They'd taken much of this stuff away for fingerprinting and whatever else they do. Then they brought it back and just put things in a heap. The Swirner people—or the people they brought in; what do you call them, stagers?—did the initial arranging." Pride flooded her face. "The first time I came in here—when Harold Swirner did me a big favor and let me in—I thought things could be shifted a little to look better."

So she had already seen the room. She did nothing to acknowledge she'd spilled those beans. Not a glint. Was she waiting for me to say I'd caught her out? I let it ride. More important matters took precedence.

"Swirner never noticed," she said. "I don't think he's that interested. He just wants to unload the place. I'm all for that. The sooner we see the last of him the better."

As she was saying this, I was looking ever more closely at the contents of the blotter. What was it I'd noticed before but had failed to take in? The folded *New York Times* took up the most space. Was it that? This time I did look at the date. Aha. It was dated only a few months earlier than the day we were there. "What's this?" I said. "This newspaper couldn't have been here back then. It's dated January twenty-sixth of this year."

"Oh, that," Ms. Belfer said. "I imagine the stager people put it there, maybe put in a new one every so often. Maybe they figure if an occupant was going to cut out something from a newspaper to put in the scrapbook, a fresh paper was called for."

The remark got me to thinking the way I hadn't when I'd first examined the room and hadn't thought to. I opened the scrapbook. The first page, made, as is standard practice, of rich green construction paper, held an obituary for someone named Carleton Stokes Hastings, who died several decades earlier. I flipped the page. Another obituary, this one for Abraham Louis Cowper. I flipped more pages. More obituaries. The scrapbook was devoted exclusively to obituaries.

It hit me that the scrapbook, the scissors, the can of

Flex Seal, the folded newspaper could only point to one thing.When Fulton Cutler's life was taken—not by himself, I reiterate—he was preparing to add a new obituary to the others. It could only be an obituary he had found in that day's edition of the *Times*—or another newspaper. Or if not that day's edition, a relatively recent edition. Yet quickly flicking through the thick pages, I determined that the last obituary Fulton Cutler had pasted into the scrapbook was dated more than a few years before the day of his death.

Two questions elbowed into my brain: (1) Were these obituaries somehow related? and (2) if Fulton Cutler were planning his suicide, wouldn't he have waited until he completed the scrapbook entry before taking his life, whereas a murderer wouldn't have any such concern?

The answer to (1) necessitated my reading, or certainly browsing, the obits to find precisely what linked them. The answer to (2) was that Fulton Cutler could not have been, as I was increasingly convinced, a suicide.

Ms. Belfer had stopped her browsing to watch me page through the obituaries. "What are you taking so much time to look at?"

"As a matter of fact, obituaries," I stated as much as inquired.

"That's depressing. Why would anyone want to collect obituaries?"

"Because," I replied, "they're more proof that no suicide took place here."

"What makes you say that?" I told her what I'd deduced about the unpasted obit. I was beginning to be impressed by what I decided was my newly acquired acumen.

Ms. Belfer screwed up her walnut-y face even walnuttier for a few seconds and then relaxed it. "I told you I always thought there was something fishy about his death." She re-screwed. "But if someone else killed him, which I don't think is what happened, what about the locked room?"

"I don't know about it yet, but there's always an explanation. I'll find it."

"What makes you think that?"

"Because the police won't think that. From what I can tell, they closed the case long ago."

"I told you so."

"And I think you're right. That's why I'm trying to find as much evidence as I can to see if they'll reopen the case." I was attempting to get her, in the politest way possible, to shut up and get back to looking at whatever she wanted to look at. I knew what I wanted to look at. "I'm going to thumb through these obits to see if there's anything that ties them together."

"More power to you," Ms. Belfer said. "I'm just going

to see if anything else needs tidying up."

She came round to the front of the desk where I was standing, opened a top right-hand drawer and pulled out a feather duster, a plastic bottle of Elmer's Glue-All and an air freshener, Febreze, of all blasted things.

She said, "At least the stagers care about keeping a place neat and tidy."

She sprayed the room with a few Febreze squirts. She seemed to favor the lemon scent. She sniffed the air, expressed satisfaction and began to dust with determined strokes.

I figured what-the-hell and pulled out the desk chair with its upholstered arms, sat down in it and picked up the scrapbook. I didn't fail to think I was sitting in the chair where Fulton Cutler was sitting when he was sent to, perhaps, a better place. I resisted leaning back to put my feet on the desk.

Instead, I opened the scrapbook again to the first obituary, noticing right away that it had been cut from the *Dayton Daily News,* first edition, August 15, 1978. It announced the Carleton Stokes Hastings death. It mentioned banker Hastings's prominent position in the community, including other organizations like "the twenty-member Fifth Street Fraternity."

The part about The Fifth Street Fraternity didn't make a strong impression on me until I had quickly skimmed the remainder of the seventeen obituaries. They were all men, all identified as a pillar of the Dayton community. Furthermore, each was also a member of The Fifth Street Fraternity. And more than one had died under suspicious circumstances.

When I'd reached the last one, short, I assumed, of the eighteenth, the one Fulton Cutler was likely about to paste in with the others, also from, I assumed, the *Dayton Daily News,* I felt obliged to wonder about several connected matters.

The *New York Times* wasn't the newspaper that should have been placed on the desk.

I'd have to do some research on that. What I'd need to do was find on what day Fulton Cutler was shot and then find the couple of days or so before that when another prominent Daytonian member of the twenty-member Fifth Street Fraternity had died.

It also occurred to me I ought to learn as much as I could about the twenty-member Fifth Street Fraternity. The way to do that was to see what anyone on the *Dayton Daily News* could tell me or, if unable to fill me in, could point me in an edifying direction. Another way to go would be to contact survivors. On that notion, I went back to three of the later obituaries and took down names. I figured they'd be the likeliest remaining surviving survivors.

Hold your horses, I said to myself but not to Ms.

Belfer. This is amounting to a load of work. Did I want to take on what bona fide police detectives should be doing? Would they do it? Perhaps in the short time I'd become aware of this clear case of injustice, I had accumulated enough questions to get actual police detectives' interest worked up again. They couldn't claim I was hallucinating.

Or could they, no matter what evidence I presented? A scrapbook of obituaries missing an obituary? That was really all I had to show and some itch about a Flex Seal can. Was that proof he could not, would not, have shot himself with a revolver he owned? Did he even own the revolver? That he did must have been looked into. Wasn't it? The word "flimsy" came nowhere near describing what I had to show.

Nope, I'd have to turn up more. Besides which, I had to confess I was excited about my new avocation. I was even impressed by my findings. Okay "flimsy" was better than nothing.

I'd search for more.

I addressed the Febreze-preoccupied Ms. Belfer. "I hope I'm not keeping you from more important things, Ms. Belfer, but I want to look at a few other...I'm going to call them clues."

"I do have other important things to do," Ms. Belfer said with more than a smidgen of grandiosity, "but I can spare another minute or two." Whether Ms. Belfer ever had genuinely important things to do was doubtful to me, if not to her.

I shut the scrapbook and got up. The two windows were my next objective. Something about them was bothering me. It wasn't anything about the garden, where no bulldog was currently presiding. What was it? I went to each of them and tried raising them again. They wouldn't budge. Investigators had to have left them that way.

But the murderer exited the room either through the windows or the door to the study, and how could he—or she—have exited through the door and locked it from outside if it only could be locked from inside? This was already hitting me as a Fulton Cutler eccentricity perhaps calling for further probing. Or not. The guy was an eccentric. Ms. Belfer had indicated as much.

Yes, I know there are ways to open from the outside a door locked from the inside. There are complicated string contrivances, for instance. But aren't they chancy? They sound that way to me.

But enough of the door, locked or not.

I had a hunch about the windows. Sure, ha! Who was I, already having more hunches? Daniel Freund, upstart snoop.

"You're looking at the windows," Ms. Belfer accurately observed. "But what good is it if you can't lift the bottom frame or lower the top one?"

How did she know that? Obviously by having tried them herself. That's how.

Was she trying to cover up her unintentional disclosure when she said, holding up the Febreze, "but I suppose I could clean them. They look like they could use a good cleaning."

With Febreze? I thought, but to humor her said, "Cleaning them, yes. Undoubtedly the right thing to do but maybe not now." I kept trying to lift or lower the window on the right, the room's west side. While doing that, I was more closely studying the wooden frames where the upper and lower frames aligned.

I noticed the semicircular metal latch was secured. Were the latch undone, the frames should be able to raise and lower. I tried the clasp. It released. I tried the lower frame. Up it went. No need to try the upper frame. I returned the latch to its closed setting, to the position it had to have been in at the time of the murder. Or had the murderer taken care of it?

What about the room's east-side window? I went to it, tried again to make it budge. No give, no give whatsoever. Then I noticed something. I was looking at the frames. I was looking at where the upper and lower frames met. What I saw gripped me. That latch wasn't closed. It could not have been. The murderer, on leaving, would have to know there would be no way to reset the latch from the outside. Furthermore, the murderer would know he (she?) had to come in through the window because he (she?) could, would more likely be seen entering and leaving the building.

Unless, of course, this was someone already in the building. How 'bout that? Already-on-the-premises suspects.

Ms. Belfer had stopped whatever she was doing—i.e., not cleaning the windows—to look at me. "What are you up to? Trying to get a breath of fresh air? I already freshened the room."

"I'm just testing the windows," I said, truthfully. Not the full truth but near enough for the moment. I was talking to myself as well as to her. "They don't open, no matter how hard I try."

"So?" Ms. Belfer queried. "They didn't then. They don't now. See? No way in or out of the room. A suicide. Swirner and Swirner probably has done nothing about any windows. Not their problem. Anybody wanting to buy a place isn't likely to make sure the windows open and close, would they?"

"I have to agree with you there, Ms. Belfer."

"Of course, you do. I'm never wrong about these things."

"Let me remind you," I slid in, "you've said, more than once, you think something fishy has gone on here."

"I still do. There was something fishy about anything and everything Fulton Cutler did."

"I know you didn't like Mr. Cutler."

"He wasn't friendly. Whenever I saw him, and I saw him often, believe you me, he wouldn't give me the time of day."

"How often did you ask him the time of day?"

She took exception to the question. "You know what I mean. He was unfriendly, but don't take my word for it. Ask the others in the building. They'll tell you the same thing."

"Mr. Cutler was disliked?"

"That's an understatement."

I had the inevitable logical next thought. "Did anyone dislike him enough to murder him?"

"You'd have to ask them."

She got that right. One of them could have figured something out. Fulton Cutler might even have asked one of them into the study at one point, one of them who'd then left without giving a hoot about either the study door or the windows that time.

If the police had concluded as swiftly as they had that there was no murder, they'd have had no reason to question other owners and tenants in the non-evict edifice about it, no reason to ask any more than the standard questions about seeing or hearing anything out of the ordinary. They'd have no reason to know Fulton Cutler was disliked.

"Say, Ms. Belfer," I inquired, again offhandedly, "did the police ever question you or any of the other people living here then about the supposed suicide?"

"They questioned every one of us. Wanted to know if anyone had heard the shot at the time the suicide was supposed to happen. We all talked to each other about it. Hardly a common thing with this crowd. Most of us do a good job of not getting in each other's way.

"I have to confess I was the one who helped the police the most. I'm the one who takes the time to do something about any problem. The others can't be bothered. But even I can't be watching the door twenty-four hours a day, for Pete's sake. Fulton Cutler, the coroner estimated, died sometime between one and four in the morning. I told them that if the suicide had taken place at a more reasonable hour, I might've been more help.

"If Fulton Cutler had told me what he planned to do, I could've suggested the early afternoon, right after lunch, is an ideal time to do yourself in. But he didn't ask me. All the years we lived here at the same time—I was here when he moved in—I think the only thing he ever asked me, no more than twice, was if the mail had arrived. Once it had. Once it hadn't.

"As for the rest of them, the only one who might have

had anything to tell them was Ed Snow, the cab driver on the top floor. He had a late shift that night, like most nights. If he'd come in sometime during it, he might have had something to say, but he said he didn't come in that night."

Something occurred to me to ascertain about this locked-room murder. The room had obviously appeared to be locked, but how had it acquired that appearance?

"Tell me, Ms. Belfer, did the police ever question you about someone entering or leaving the building at the time of the murder—at the time of the so-called suicide?"

"Why would they? Who would be visiting at that time of night? If anyone had, what would that have to do with a suicide? Anyway, no one without keys could get in unless they were let in, and no one was up that late at night to let anyone in. Except Ed Snow, who wasn't here and says he had the tabs to prove it. Which you wouldn't check anyway for a suicide."

Nor, I reminded myself, could anyone have left by the front door, the study door having been locked from the inside. How 'bout that? Where does that leave on-the-premises suspects? Could someone contrive a way to lock it from the outside? String, a small pliers, something like a hairpin?

It hadn't yet gotten late in the afternoon, but I'd been on the prowl for several hours. It was time to reconnoiter. The study was getting claustrophobic. I venture to say it had plenty to do with the unfortunate events that had transpired in it closing down on me, if not on Ms. Belfer. I said to her, "We've been here long enough. We can go. I've gotten a good look at the room. Or maybe you want to stay."

"I've had enough of this," Ms. Belfer said. Was she aware that she'd just quoted Fulton Cutler's supposed suicide note? If so, she didn't accompany it with any sort of walnut-wink.

Which got me to thinking. If there had been no suicide, there would have been no suicide note. Any suicide note would have had to be placed there by the murderer. But it was on Fulton Cutler's stationery. Unless it was fake stationery, some facsimile run up by the murderer. But how would a murderer have access to Fulton Cutler's stationery? There was a poser. Maybe it was some sort of associate who'd been there before and made off with a sheet when Fulton Cutler wasn't looking. But no. The police with the suicide verdict had to have verified Fulton Cutler's handwriting.

"Just a sec, Ms. Belfer." She was already at the door to the once locked, I mean, to the shiftily once-secured room. "There's one last thing I want to do."

She stood where she was, annoyed, while I went around to the front of the desk. I pulled open the center drawer, which, by the way, featured a keyhole but held no key. Maybe Fulton Cutler locked it sometimes, maybe not. Maybe that key was also missing. It wasn't. It was the first thing I saw in the drawer. Something, that is, looking like a desk key would look.

The second thing I saw was a stack of Fulton Cutler stationery. Had someone had the opportunity to help himself or herself? Would a murderer intent on getting in and out fast take the time to force Fulton Cutler to pull out stationery and, a gun pointed at his head, take dictation.

Possible but hardly likely.

Shuffling around, I found matching envelopes and the usual desk drawer contents—pens, pencils, a pencil sharpener, paper clips, five letters addressed to Mr. Fulton Cutler.

I recognized the return addresses very likely were those of Fifth Street Fraternity members. I replaced the letters, thinking I'd read them next time Ms. Belfer let me into the room.

My major takeaway from this second look was that the note found at the crime scene was written by Fulton Cutler. It had to have been. That was the major takeaway. There were others milling around in my head I hadn't sorted out.

With my next project in mind, I shut the drawer, reopened it, picked up the key I assumed was the key to the drawer, shut the drawer again, inserted the key in the keyhole and promptly locked and unlocked the drawer.

Interesting that the drawer had not been locked. Did it mean that Fulton Cutler had a habit of leaving things unlocked, things like the door to the room? If Cutler had been murdered, which—needless to say again, he was—the murderer most likely had locked the room one way or another and might even be the one in possession of the now missing key to the door.

Unless the police were still in possession of it, with Fulton Cutler's fingerprints on it and no one else's.

This was something to be dealt with later. Right now, I wanted to see about something else.

"Did you find what you were looking for?" Ms. Belfer asked. I could see she was even more eager to get going, her other self-imposed tenant obligations, doncha know? There were other building occupants to keep an eye on and watch out for, not to mention strangers like me wanting to scrutinize the building for legitimate or illegitimate purposes.

A wary woman's work is never done.

Her need was, as it happened, in line with mine. I answered her question. "Yes, I found what I was looking for. What I want to ask you about, as you suggested, are the other people living here."

Wouldn't I have to consider each of them at the very least a person of interest, I think the phrase is? Though I might not put it like that to Ms. Belfer. Any one of them could have committed the crime without being seen entering or leaving the building, as if anyone had even bothered to ask at the time the nasty deed was investigated.

"The day Fulton Cutler died, Ms. Belfer, you said it was sometime between one and four in the morning. Then tell me this. During those three hours, did you hear any sound like a gunshot?"

"The police asked me that, and everyone else in the building. I said no. Who remembers everything they heard over three hours? Not in this neighborhood, anyway. Even in the wee hours when horns can still be honking and car radios blasting and people screaming in the street and sirens wailing and cats screeching."

"But Ms. Belfer, don't you live in the back of the building? Do you hear all that noise back there?"

Ms. Belfer pulled the day's flannel number tighter around her. "Sometimes I have trouble sleeping and sit here on the stoop. You'd be surprised what goes on, even at four in the morning. Maybe even the four in the morning we're talking about when I wasn't having trouble sleeping. Maybe that kind of noise drowned out Fulton Cutler ending it all."

She had it right about the frequent wee-hours noise. My building right down the street, where I live second floor front, is a testament to her description.

"You don't remember hearing anything?"

"Like I said, I didn't hear a thing. And my bedroom was right above the locked room. Sometimes I can be a heavy sleeper. I'd like to sleep with one eye open, but I can't."

I pictured Ms. Belfer's bed, an end table next to it, on it an almost empty beer bottle and an atomizer with which she liberally sprayed on Lilies of the Valley. I kept the fragrant image to myself and said, "What about anyone else in the building?"

"I can tell you they didn't."

"You did suggest I ask them, Ms. Belfer. I think I'll do that. I would appreciate your telling me who they are. Were." Then for no reason other than my own pleasure I had another playful bout. "That's assuming you know them."

"I'm acquainted with them," she said, dismissively. "There aren't that many. Mostly renters. Including me, four of us are still here. This is a non-evict co-op, you know. The first floor is empty. Fulton Cutler was a co-op owner, and I'm on the second floor. Not a co-op owner. There's a young guy in the front, a tall, skinny guy. Donny Prager, he calls himself. I think he's some kind of personal trainer or something, whatever they're up to. But he's only been living here a few weeks. Not worth asking."

That had to be the Ichabod Crane guy I buttonholed the previous day. I could rule him out, but what about the previous tenant or tenants in that apartment?

"The same goes for the people in the ground-floor apartment," Ms. Belfer was expatiating. "They moved in not too long after Fulton Cutler died. They never knew him. Whether they knew anything about him I couldn't say. They're a married couple, the Hilliards, both lawyers—and co-opers. They've told me that much about themselves. No children, unless you count the dog, the bulldog Champ, who gets the run of the yard. A nice yard, too. You saw it when you were looking out the windows. I see it out my windows. Far as I know, they clean up after it, after Champ." She underlined "Champ" with a sneer. "What is it with bulldogs? You see a lot of them, them and dachshunds, and what do you call the others? Jack Russells. Now the only ones left are the people living on the third and fourth floors. They're not my favorites, either. Third floor front, Mr. Winger, who does heaven-knows-what. Keeps to himself mostly, maybe because he has to. You see him when he takes his bike in and out. It's one of the kind you can fold up. He told me the name of it, the brand, I mean—Bromley or Bromkin, something like that. You ask me, he's getting too old to ride a bike, the way they ride them in the streets these days. Menaces. But far be it from me to say anything to him about it. I don't even know his first name. Don't bother to check the mailbox. It's not there. Only Winger. Who's he hiding from? He was here when Cutler was, not that I ever saw them say as much as boo to each other.

"So was third floor back, Miss Pritchard, here then. Amy Pritchard. She teaches dance at someplace like Arthur Murray or Fred Astaire, if those places still exist. I could swear she teaches at home, too. The gentleman callers. I can't say I ever saw anyone go up there or leave that looked like they want to rumba or tango, unless horizontally. But why else do I hear such thumping over my head? Not at one to four in the morning, mind. I've talked to her about it. Does it do any good? Still thump-thump-thump. Night after night. Fulton Cutler wasn't the only one here where something fishy was going on.

"Same for fourth floor front, Jason Arnold, a painter, is there now. He says he needs northern light. He's been here at least two years, and I have yet to see a single painting. A' course, he wasn't here when Fulton Cutler got his. A person calling himself George Reiser moved in when old lady Cooper died up there. Of natural causes. Poor thing. That Mr. Reiser was a weird one—stayed in days and only went out at night. To do nothing I could ever get him to talk about. Maybe he was a night watchman.

As good a guess as any. Not Fulton Cutler's hours at all, but, like I said, he was here at the suicide or the whatever you think you're calling it. Left not too much after. If you're looking for a mysterious somebody, he's one for you. Hoo-boy. When he moved out, I asked him where he was going. 'Heading west,' he said. What kind of answer is that? The others are easy enough to grab. I don't have any idea how to reach George Reiser. You're on your own there.

"Then there's fourth floor rear, Ed Snow. Drives a cab, l told you. He's quite the ladies' man. Ha. That's how he fancies himself. I can tell you different. I don't see any parade of girls coming and going. What I do see is the dirty magazines sticking out of his back pockets. He was living here when Fulton Cutler was whatever he was. Murdered. Suicided.

"That's all I can tell you. It's not much, but I have things to do other than stand here all day long gabbing with you."

Having delivered her monologue at a breathless pace, she made no move to move. I was not inclined to stop her throughout the discourse. If I had, she might have taken offense and clammed up. And I was learning plenty. The only challenge was keeping track of which occupant was which and which had been living in the building when Fulton Cutler was done in.

If I had it right, the Hilliards downstairs weren't. Neither were Donny Prager, the personal trainer on the second floor, or Jason Arnold, the painter on the fourth floor. That left both Mr. Winger, who kept to himself; dance teacher, Amy Pritchard, on the third floor; cab driver Snow fourth floor back and long-gone George Reiser fourth floor front. Would any of them have anything like a strong motivation?

No need to point out—she'd pointed it out herself—that Ms. Belfer occupied the second-floor rear. That's when she bothered to fill space there and not on the stoop.

I'm eliminating her, although I'm not certain I should. Maybe I should, after all. She was too convinced it was a suicide. If she were the murderer, I think she'd have been so pleased with herself, she would have found a way to let it slip, even boast about it, bless her nosy little heart.

As prime suspects, I had to eliminate the Hilliards, the trainer and the painter. The others I would have to suss out, as, it hit me, I'd have to track the previous tenant(s) in the Hilliard apartment and the trainer's.

I reckoned I could forget about poor old lady Cooper, who likely had not come back from the dead to off Fulton Cutler.

Did I mention that during Ms. Belfer's thorough, if long-winded, soliloquy we'd returned to the stoop? I noticed that all the discarded books were gone. I'm glad I got there when I did.

Or am I? That pushy 1953 *Great Gatsby* edition.

"Ms. Belfer," I asked, as she leaned against the open outer door, flannel whatever held customarily tight, "I think I might want to talk soon to the ones in the building who were here then and still are. No time to lose."

"I can do better than tha—," she started to say but stopped. "What was I thinking? I totally forgot another one who was here then but isn't now. Raoul Paget." She pronounced the first name *Rah-ool* and the surname *Pah-jhay.* "Look, I can't be expected to remember every-thing." She looked at me as if I'd insisted she must. "I have enough other things to think about. But how could I have forgotten him? Raoul Paget?"

I skipped her swipe at my imagined demands and said, "*Rah-ool Pah-jhay?*"

"Yes, p-a-g-e-t. French. *Rah-ool Pah-jhay.* God forbid I said *Padg-ette.* It was *Pah-jhay.* Don't get me started on the *Rah-ool* part. Anyway, he was the one living opposite me when Fulton Cutler did the you-know-what. Shortly after that, he went to San Francisco. He didn't say right away where he was moving. I had to worm it out of him, which is something I don't like to do. He was a chef. But you don't think he had anything to do with the crime. Assuming there was a crime, which I'm not. If he was going to kill somebody, he'd do it with one of his kitchen knives, don't you think?"

That was a piece of logic I'd deal with later.

Just then Ms. Belfer was uncustomarily silenced by a man exiting the building, wearing spattered overalls and carrying what could be taken for a frame.

As he sped down the stoop past us, Ms. Belfer said, "Hello, Mr. Arnold" and gave me a walnut-wink. Under her breath, she said to me, "Jason Arnold, the, uh, painter."

Jason Arnold mumbled something incomprehensible and kept going.

"See what I mean," Ms. Belfer said. I didn't.

Not a problem since she merrily resumed with yet another forgotten Fulton Cutler contemporary. "Before the Hilliards took possession of their place, the guy living there and gone now was C. F. Congdon. Don't ask me what the 'F' was for. Who knows, who cares?"

She enjoyed that notion and then said, "Well, lookee-lookee, if it isn't Ed Snow heading our way."

I looked right and left and saw only a few feet away a heavyset balding man of about fifty-five dressed in a denim shirt and khaki trousers with a red bandana tied around his neck, a battered leather cap. His face was ruddy. His thick stubble looked as if it hadn't been shaved in a day or three. At first blush he didn't resemble the ladies' man Ms. Belfer said he claimed to be. Not at second blush, either.

He started up the stoop and said without much enthusiasm, "Ms. Belfer." He completely ignored me as he pulled keys out of a pants pocket.

Ms. Belfer stood her ground. "Mr. Snow. You might want to meet Mr. Freund here. He's writing a book on unsolved murders in New York City and wants to talk to us."

Ed Snow stopped on the top step next to Ms. Belfer. "What's that got to do with me or you? Far as I know, there's been no murder here. There've been times I thought about it." He gave Ms. Belfer a sharp look. "Far as I know, there's just been the suicide. Whatsisname."

"Fulton Cutler," Ms. Belfer supplied.

"Yeah, him."

"Mr. Freund here thinks it was a murder."

Ed Snow showed some interest. "What makes him think that?" he said to Ms. Belfer, then turned to me on the step just below her, "What makes you think that? Cops said it was open-and-shut. The suicide note and all. The no fingerprints but his on the gun."He gave me a harder look—I practically felt it—as if he thought I was nominating him. "If they thought it was a murder, they would've asked all of us here, ain't that right?"

Ms. Belfer asserted herself. "They did question us."

"Not as suspects. As, you know, witnesses. I had my alibi. I don't mean alibi. I mean, where I was at the time, or where I was at the time they think it all happened. You know, if we heard anything, anything that sounded like a gunshot. I didn't hear anything. I couldn't. I wasn't even here during the time they said he bumped himself off. I was taking a night shift that night, and I had my pickups to prove it."

Thinking how I thought a valid detective would think, I said, "Couldn't you have come back here at some time between pickups? I'm just speculating."

"Listen, buddy, keep your speculating to yourself. Anyways, that night I never was anywhere near here till I come back after the sun was up, when whatsisname wasn't even found yet. I remember that, and that's what I told the cops. They could check me out. If I'd realized it was anything like a murder, I probably would'nta minded. I never liked the guy, what little I saw of him. Whenever I did, he looked me up and down as if he didn't like what he saw. Who was he? One time I said to him, 'What are you looking at?' You know what he said? 'Not much.' Howdya like that? 'Not much.' Who did he think he was? Some rich mucky-muck. I gotta say I wasn't surprised when he did himself in. If I was him, I mighta done the same thing."

Spoken like a guy who would not have minded if Fulton Cutler had been done in. He'd just said as much. But,

I thought to myself, not spoken like a guy who was the likely doer-inner. Nobody who'd committed a murder would talk so freely about committing murder. For the moment and for probably longer I could cross him off the suspects list.

Time for Ms. Belfer to put her two cents in. "You don't mean that, Ed, about him."

"Don't I?" Ed Snow snickered. "I get them in my cab all the time. Think they're better than the rest of us. Except when it comes to tips. The richer they are, the smaller the tip. I'd like to do them all in. Or maybe just one to stand for all the others." He turned to me, "Now if you don't mind, buster, I gotta get upstairs. Big night tonight."

With that, he gave me what I took to be his idea of a tough guy-womanizer look and pushed past us. As he did, I got a view of his back pockets. A rolled magazine stuck out of the left one.

When he'd let himself through the inner door, Ms. Belfer said, "Not the nicest, Ed Snow, but he always pays his rent on time. I know that for a fact."

I wondered what other debts he might pay if he thought he'd been provoked enough. I let the thought go, supposing instead I might linger on the stoop in hopes another of the supposed in-house suspects would show. But no, I had a few things I needed to think over.

I'd had the pleasure of Ms. Belfer's company long

enough as well. It had gotten later in the afternoon. I said, "Thanks for your help, Ms. Belfer, but I better get going."

"Are you giving up on your farfetched idea about Fulton Cutler and murder? Isn't it enough already?"

"Not by a long shot," I said.

"That's funny," Ms. Belfer said. "'Not by a long shot.'"

"I didn't mean it that way."

"That's the way it came out."

I wasn't going to win this exchange, but, I figured, let the inconsequential things go. "It couldn't have been a long shot, Ms. Belfer. For it to look like a suicide, the murderer would have had to shoot smack up against Mister Cutler's temple. Now I really must be going. Goodbye, Ms. Belfer."

She said goodbye, but I wasn't waiting for it. I realized as I left for my building that if I walked toward it—to the left, that is—she could be maintaining her watch on me. I turned right toward Eighth Avenue and rounded the corner. And now what? I'd have to peek to see when and if she abandoned her post. Who knew how long this might take? Keeping up this little ruse about where I didn't live was going to get old quickly.

I'd think of something.

In the meantime, I snuck a look back. As luck would have it, Ms. Belfer was gone.

I started for home, but I had another idea.

I live on the south side of the block between Eighth and Ninth Avenues. On the south side of the block between Eighth and Seventh Avenues, that's the Tenth police precinct. Why not drop in? Before I'd gotten into the supposed locked room, I'd rejected the impulse. I thought presenting the strangely behaving *Great Gatsby* 1953 edition would only prompt belly laughs, which might have been momentous from cops with big bellies.

I pictured myself handing my hyperactive edition to a desk sergeant or one of the detectives, possibly even a detective who'd been on the case. I pictured asking one or both to read just the first page. What if nothing happened when someone other than I did that? What if something did? Where would I be then? Tossed out on my ear might be the least painful result.

But now I'd been in the room and my instincts might elicit some long-dismissed interest, even if I couldn't put my finger on the implications of any of them. But maybe bringing up the obits or even, for a lark, Flex Seal.

The circumstances had earlier seemed conclusively pointing to suicide—"the suicide note and all that," as Ed Snow had phrased it, "the no fingerprints on the gun" that weren't Fulton Cutler's.

So it's likely even the mere question of murder had never arisen. Perhaps raising the slim possibility of it now might get some moderate attention.

Of course, I wouldn't say anything about how I came to be interested. I'd say nothing about the word-trampolining 1953 *Great Gatsby* object. I'm not that dense. I'd just say I knew someone in the building and had gone into the still unsold apartment where little had been changed since the obviously conscientious police scrutiny. I was simply wondering.

Getting all this straight in my mind, I'd reached the couple of metal barriers in front of the precinct. A handful of cops of different shapes, sizes, colors and genders were shooting the breeze on the precinct steps. I headed toward them. One of the assembled asked if they could be of any help.

"I hope so," I said. "I have a question about a crime committed in the neighborhood a few years back."

Another one asked, "And which one is that?" He looked at the others. They all exchanged looks that translated as "today's loony."

I disregarded the silent group comment and said, "Maybe some of you remember it. It was a suicide in the next block, a man by the name of Fulton Cutler."

The looks the cops gave each other then was more of the does-that-mean-anything-to-you variety. One cocked his head and spoke. "Oh, yeah, I remember it. I don't think any of the rest of you was here. A suicide. Open-and-shut case. Locked room, suicide note. Only the dead man's fingerprints on a .38 revolver, if I remember right."

He turned to me. "What do you want to know about it?"

I foolishly said, "Don't laugh at me, but I think it might have been a murder."

I shouldn't have to relate that that was their cue to exchange get-this-one looks, accompanied by abundant eyes rolls.

"You do, huh," the vet remarked, "and what makes you think that?"

He was humoring me for the pleasure of his cronies, but I pressed on. My first-year P. I. convictions, you know. "I've been in the room, and it just didn't feel right."

Another one chimed in. "Now that's interesting. How did you get into the room, and what didn't feel right? We'd like to know."

A second round of eye rolls.

Even as I answered, I had the premonition I shouldn't have. "I know a tenant in the building."

That's when another of them said with an outright wink at the others, "That wouldn't be a Ms. Belfer, would it?"

More today's-loony looks. There was a chorus of "Ms. Belfer"s as he added, "Does Ms. Belfer believe the Fulton Cutler suicide was a murder, too?"

"No," I said.

Another asked but waggishly, "How did she come to let you in the room?" He showily inserted his tongue in his cheek. "Are you some kind of gumshoe on the case?"

I regrouped. "No, I'm just interested."

A different one asked, "How did you get to be interested? Who are you, and what do you really do?"

There are times when honesty may not be the best policy. "I'm Daniel Freund. I'm a writer."

"Fiction?" the vet asked, amid more looks. I could only nod assent. "Sounds, friend, like you're dreaming up more of it."

There are times when the word "friend" isn't used in friendship. This qualified.

The crack reaped hearty laughs from his colleagues, all of whom also gave the impression they dealt with things of this nature on a regular basis.

The vet wasn't through with me. He said, "But if you have new information on the case, you might want to speak to the desk sergeant inside." I was surprised at his suggestion for the split second it took me to understand he was cooking up more entertainment for the others—and for the desk sergeant and anyone else within earshot.

I thanked him with more abashment than I would have liked, and, with him leading the way and the others following behind me, I was led through the large double doors and past a cop sitting at a reception post. He received what I figured was some sort of knowing smirk.

Then I was facing a desk sergeant. That's to say, I was facing up, as if pleading, and he was facing down, as if categorizing.

The vet told his superior that I was Daniel Freund, a fiction writer and that I had a question about a case the precinct handled some years before. Out of the corner of my eye I thought I saw one of the other cops circle an index finger aside his right temple—close enough to where a right-handed suicide would hold a .38.

"And what case would that be?" the desk sergeant asked, signaling to the others he was already in on the joke.

I decided that as a sign of sincerity and, even more substantial than that, *compos mentis,* I would be concise. "The suicide death of Fulton Cutler about three years ago."

The sergeant made a show of giving it thought. He tilted his head up and closed his eyes momentarily in feigned thought. He went so far as to scratch his cleft chin. "Yes," he said, stretching the "yes" for about a yard, "I remember that case. That's the man who took his life in a locked room. An open-and-shut case if I recall correctly. And what's your question about it?"

I acted as if I had not noticed his attitude. "It's not so much a question as a statement."

"Your statement is?"

"I have reason to believe it may not have been a suicide."

To keep his fellow officers tickled, the sergeant was still going along with me, "That's very interesting. Did you say your name is Freund?"

I hadn't said it. The vet officer had, but I wasn't going to contradict the sergeant who had me at a few disadvantages. One was that he was looking down at me as if jollying himself from a great height.

I only said, "Daniel Freund."

"Daniel Freund. Well, Mister Freund—." I wondered whether it was police etiquette to address civilians by their surnames. To my dismay, most people these days immediately on introduction skip to first names. "—you must know that the victim, Fulton Cutler, was discovered in a locked room with a suicide note on his desk and a weapon, a Magnum .38 revolver, on the floor by his hand. That's how I remember it. I was on the force then but still a cop on the beat. I didn't have much to do with the case. I think I was stationed outside the Cutler building a few times during the couple days before we closed the case. Satisfactorily. I did get to know a Ms. Belfer, I think her name was, who lived there. By any chance, do you know her?"

I nodded I did.

One of the other cops behind me chimed in with, "She's still there, awright."

The sergeant took this in and went on, "But I remember it was pretty much considered an open-and-shut case. You don't think so?"

I surmised what was called for then was my being deferential. "No, sergeant—."

"Sergeant Brian Doyle," he filled in.

"Sergeant Doyle, I've been in that room, and I think there are some suspicious details that should be looked at again." I considered what I was saying. "You may not know that not too much has been changed in the room from that day. The apartment has been on the market since then but hasn't sold."

Sergeant Doyle said, "Mr. Freund, the police aren't so much interested in buildings for their commercial value. It's criminal activity in them that takes up our time."

"I understand that," I said, maintaining the position that I intended to engage in a straightforward conversation. "That's why I think it might be a good idea to reopen the case."

"Reopen an open-and-shut case," he stated in mock thought and aimed another gaze not only at the officers who'd escorted me in but at several others who'd collected collegially in the large institutional room with its seasick-gray-green walls, heavy air and antiseptic aroma.

Hoping to stay on forthright ground, I said, "Reopen the case or at the very least—."

He repeated, "At the very least—." The cops got a kick out of that.

I pretended to continue disregarding them, and, growing bold at my peril, I added, "Or perhaps you'd allow me to look at the records to ascertain the day of death and things like that."

A chorus of dissonant chuckles, snickers and titters ensued.

The sergeant said, "I'm afraid I couldn't do that, Mr. Freund, not even the day the suicide was discovered." He looked around. "Do any of you old-timers"—that said with a bushy eyebrow raised—"remember the date? Or anything close to it?"

The vet from outside said, "Nah. Who remembers dates?" He stroked his shaved chin. "Oh, yeah. I'd say it was sometime in the spring, about this time of year. Maybe sometime in May, warmer."

Doyle showed only mild annoyance at the vet's speaking up. "Okay, there's some information for you, but we just can't open our records to anyone who walks in off the street, no matter how persuasive they are about what they think they know. We have too much to do here to find time reviewing closed cases. You might not think it from what's going on right now."

He gazed around at the cops getting idle laughs from the way he was handling me, figuratively manhandling me. "We just can't do it. Not even for a fiction writer like yourself. Come to think of it, you didn't tell me if you write mysteries."

"I don't."

"Glad to hear it, Mister Freund. Most mystery writers get police work all wrong. Just my opinion. But I'll tell you what I'll do. The next best thing to reopening the case or just the report. I'm going to give you the name of the detectives who handled the case for us—Detective Sergeant Izzy Abramovitz and Detective Sergeant Patrick Dugan." The names evoked renewed murmurs and one or two random sniggers from some of those trying to act as if they weren't listening intently.

"Oh, yeah, Abramovitz," the vet chuckled. "Just the one to help Mr. Freund here."

Additional chuckles emerged.

"Abramovitz," Sergeant Doyle continued, as if unaware of the others, "has since retired, but he may still be in the city. Dugan's retired, too. He's in Florida somewhere. Some of the officers here knew them, and others didn't." He looked around at his crew. "Okay, you slackers, back to it."

Then, while the slackers worked at working but kept me under supervision, not to say, suspicion, he said, "You'll have to track them down yourself. Abramovitz lives in Brooklyn or did. He said he wanted to retire to someplace on the shore. Maybe he did, maybe he didn't. I used to have his phone numbers here." He pulled a book from the left side of a pile of papers on his stacked desk and thumbed through it. "Apparently, I don't."

I couldn't determine whether he was telling the truth.

"But Izzy—real name Israel, never used around here—might want to talk to you." A few outright guffaws greeted this. Doyle paid no mind. "Whatever else he was—." I heard a few titters. "—he's the kind of guy who when he gets convinced of something is hard to get around. If you find him, you better be prepared to be talked out of whatever you think went on with Cutler." Doyle shifted and even altered his attitude toward me. "That's all I can tell you, Mister Freund."

He gave me a little wave of the downturned fingers on his right hand. "Thanks for dropping by. I wish we saw more concerned citizens here." I was being summarily dismissed—and dismissed without ever having said the words "Flex Seal" or "obits." The last words he imparted were, "Hey, Mr. Freund, do me a favor and give Ms. Belfer my warm regards."

I nodded I would and turned around. The cop flank separated into two rows. I walked through, and as I left, one of them held the inner door open for me and several others echoed Sergeant Doyle's regards to Ms. Belfer.

Back on the street, I consulted my watch. It was

already almost four o'clock. I'd had a busy day. I had better return to the apartment to think through my next moves. By the time I got there, I fixed on getting in touch with Israel "Izzy" Abramovitz and then talking to the two remaining relevant tenants down the block.

Not that I expected them to be much help, although one of them could have been holding an intense grudge against Fulton Cutler and, in his or her fervor, might have sketched out the locked-room ruse.

That had to be looked into. Who knew what I might discover? Then and posthaste, I'd contact the previous tenants living on the premises when Fulton Cutler said "Howya doin'?" to his maker.

Maybe it was just instinct, but I hung on to my belief that the resolutely regarded open-and-shut case may have not been that but would turn out to be—is it usually termed?—an inside case.

At home, after assuring myself Ms. Belfer wasn't at her usual lemonade stand, I made myself an early dinner and, having finished it, sat in my reading chair. I didn't turn on the lamp. Neither did I pick up the Hal Siegel *Great Gatsby* edition I'd left on the end table. I feared the invisible hand. I didn't want it perp-walking me through the novel again.

Not unless somewhere in there was the murderer's identity, and if that were so, wouldn't the hand have

already led me to it, perhaps to a succession of single letters adding up to the criminalizing (is one obliged to add
"alleged"?) name?

Ruminating on all of this, I was interrupted by a flapping noise. I looked at the end table. Siegel 1953 was rest-
lessly flapping its cover. "Get on with it," I thought I heard
it prompting in a husky voice more Tom Buchanan's than
how I'd always imagined Nick Carraway's would sound.

So I took the locked-room facts clouding my brain
to bed with me early. I didn't immediately fall asleep. I
didn't toss and turn physically, only mentally. I thought I
was on to something. I thought I wasn't on to something.

When I eventually lost consciousness with no new
aperçus affecting me, I dreamed not about Fulton Cutler
and his dubious demise but about one of the old reliables,
the one about being back at college freshman year and
not knowing where to find my first class.

WEDNESDAY

I woke up at about nine and even before I put on any clothes, it came to me that if the cocky Tenth Precinct squad was going to be no help, maybe Izzy Abramovitz would be. I had to concede that help of any sort couldn't hurt. I'd show that self-satisfied bunch.

I went to my computer and googled Izzy Abramovitz. There he was, plain as day, listed in Brooklyn on Nostrand Avenue.

Izzy Abramovitz—if this was the right Izzy Abramovitz—still had a landline. Was nine in the morning too early to call? Surely not for a cop, even for an ex-cop. To be on the safe side, I wolfed some cereal until 9:30 and dialed the number.

(Why do we still call it dialing when dialing has nothing to do with it? Yet one more mystery for another time.)

The phone rang twice before a man picked up the phone and shouted, "Yeah, whaddaya want?"

The volume set me back, but I plowed on, "Excuse me for interrupting you—."

"Yeah, you interrupted my breakfast, which some people think is the best meal of the day. I don't. Not the way I cook. The way I cook there is no best meal of the day. Whaddaya want?"

"I'm trying to reach Israel Abramovitz, Izzy Abramovitz. Are you by any chance—?"

"Maybe I am, maybe I'm not. Whaddaya want 'im for?" I'm usually not that easily intimidated, but if this exchange is anything to go by, maybe I am. "If this is the Izzy Abramovitz who was a police detective with the Tenth Precinct in Manhattan, I would like to talk to him—you—him about a case he investigated a few years ago."

"I investigated many cases a few years ago."

"Then you are Izzy Abramovitz?"

"Didn't I just say so?" He hadn't exactly, but I wasn't up to quibbling. "What case is that, and who wants to know?" The gruff basso profundo voice had become gravelly, like tires riding over crushed stones.

"My name is Daniel Freund, and—."

"I don't know any Daniel Freund. If you're trying to sell me something, I ain't buying."

"Please believe me, sir, I'm not selling anything."

"Don't sir me. I'm not an officer. I was a detective sergeant and proud of it. The only thing I didn't like about it was being sirred. Save it for the military."

"I understand, Mr. Abramovitz, excuse me. I'm calling you because I'm interested in a suicide you investigated. A man named Fulton Cutler."

"That case. Yeah, I remember it. One of the easiest cases I ever had. Open-and-shut. Whaddaya wanna know about it at this hour of the mornin'?"

Although I wondered how an ex-police detective who'd undoubtedly been hauled from bed at all hours of the day and night would be bothered by a phone call at ten o'clock in the morning, I kept it to myself. Maybe in his retirement he was making up for all the three a.m. roustings.

As I did with Sergeant Doyle, I went right to my point. "I'm calling you because I recently had Mr. Cutler's death brought to my attention." I hoped he wouldn't ask what had caused this. He didn't. Not then, anyway. I hurried on. "I know it was believed to be an open-and-shut case—."

"Not *believed* to be open-and-shut," Izzy Abramovitz cut in. "*Proved* to be an open-and-shut case. Within minutes of walking into the previously locked room, I knew everything about Cutler's case added up to it. I was in charge of the case with Patrick Dugan, that half-wit, and I came to my conclusion before you could say Jack Robinson. Or Lebron James. Matter of fact, it was one of the easiest cases I ever dealt with in a long, sometimes pretty nauseatin' career. When you've seen enough of death in any number of circumstances, you learn to call a spade a spade right off the bat."

I was in the phone presence of a man happily not

averse to clichés. Okay, there are truths in clichés, and I was after the truth.

He steamrolled on. "The number of cases I was working on at the time means you can't afford to waste time on the obvious ones. Is that what you wanted to hear? Nothin' else about the Cutler case could qualify as an excuse to keep me from my scrambled eggs."

"If you'll forgive me, Mister Abramovitz," I said, hearing an intimidated tone I wanted to dispel, "but I think I have some credible reasons to think that maybe Fulton Cutler's death wasn't suicide."

"Sufferin' succotash. What do you think it was? Natural causes? You're right. If a man holds a double-action .38 to his head and fires it, it natur'ly causes death."

"That's not what I'm saying," I said.

"What the fuck are you sayin'? And you better say it quick."

I stone-cold got the impression I'd better say it quick. Guided at the same time by an impulse to downplay, I said, "I think it was murder."

"Murder!" Abramovitz brayed into the phone. I don't think that if he could have forced his arm through the line to grab me by the throat, he wouldn't have. "Who are you, anyway? Don't tell me. Some pipsqueak private dick with no clients at the moment and nothing else to do but try to make a great big somethin' outta a great big nothin'."

"Uh, no," I started, "I'm not a private detective. I guess you could say I'm a concerned citizen with some doubts."

"For fuck's sake, don't pull any concerned citizen crap on me. I had my fill of that when I was on the force. There's nothin' worse than a concerned citizen standin' in your way when you're tryin' to get a case solved. What, you're gonna tell me you somehow got innerested in the Cutler thing and have found evidence I never took into account?"

"That's not exactly it," I said. That was exactly it. I was flailing to buy time.

"I got it," he said, raising his decibel level, which I might have said was impossible. "You're one of those crackpots convinced for some dumbass reason that Fulton Cutler was murdered. He wasn't. Period. The end. Are you through now?"

"One of those crackpots"? This surprised me. Could there be somebody else who got hold of the murdered man's *Great Gatsby* copy before me and was subjected to the same combustible pyrotechnics I'd been?

"You mean," I pondered, "there's somebody else who thinks Fulton Cutler didn't take his own life?"

"Not that one. Close to every other case I ever worked on there's always some nut job who thinks he knows better. Or she does. Generally, I trust women more than men."

Time for me to get aggressive, too. "And they were all wrong?"

"Whaddaya think? Every one of them was way wrong. You don't fool a fooler. I suppose you think you can. I'd like to know what makes you think so, how you got involved with a closed case so old it's got whiskers a yard long."

I wasn't about to tell him about the tsk-tsking *TGG* edition I'd found on Fulton Cutler's former stoop. "I-uh-I-I-uh—."

"Spit it out, man."

"As I said, I managed to get in the room, which hasn't been much changed since the-uh-the-uh...event. That's the way they do things these days when they're trying to sell a place. And I just think there may have been a few things you could have overlooked."

"I overlo—!"

"That may be the wrong word. A few things that might...that might look different to you now."

"I doubt it," Izzy Abramovitz said, subduing his tone only slightly, "but that case is beginning to come back to me more clearly now. Tell me this, that's the one in the buildin' where that weird woman—what's 'er name?— thinks it's her job to play prison warden. I don't remember her name."

"Ms. Belfer."

"That's her. The whole time we were conducting the investigation she was some pain in the ass. You're gonna tell me she has somethin' to do with this *meshugenah* phone call?"

"I suppose I am," I said, supposing the truth might reap benefits. "She did help me gain access to Fulton Cutler's study."

"You're tryin' not to say locked room, but that's what it was, no goddam question."

"I'm not questioning if it was locked. I'm sure it was locked. In my opinion—."

"Has anyone asked your opinion?" Izzy Abramovitz wanted to know.

I wasn't going to tell him that a series of bouncing, incandescing words and a phantom hand that might have belonged to the spirit of F. Scott Fitzgerald asked not so much for my opinion as for my speedy action.

"Not really, but I'm sure the room was locked. If Mister Cutler hadn't locked it himself, the murderer would have locked it for his or her own purposes of making the death look like a suicide. Yes, I buy that the room was locked. What I think is worth considering is that there may be other ways to leave a locked room than through the door."

"You know what, Mister Freund. You're right. If Santa Claus can get himself down the chimney and out again, a murderer can, too." He lowered his voice a tad. "Why didn't I think of that?" He raised it many additional tads. "Except in that room there was no fireplace. There was no chimney. So what did this mysterious murderer of yours do? Shrink himself or herself into an inch tall or compress into gas and slide under the door, then get life-size again? I don't think so."

"No, but maybe even through the door, if he or she thought up some clever way to relock it from the outside."

"Mister Freund," Izzy Abramovitz said, "you read too many books and watch too much television. *Law & Order* this ain't."

I didn't deem it the appropriate time to say I'd been watching the long-running series for years and many series like it and had learned only too well from them that a locked-room suicide has to be a locked-room murder.

"How about the windows?" I asked with as much conviction as I had left in my quiver, "quiver" a word with at least two meanings. I was in the throes of both.

"Now you're goin' so far out on a limb you're losin' your grip. If you really gave the room more than a once-over, you know the windows were locked as tight as the door. We couldn't force them no matter how hard we tried."

I hurried in with, "Don't you think there's something funny about that?"

"Faulty windows in a New York City building? There's nothing funny about it. Don't just ask me. Ask millions of New York *shlubs* fighting with their windows on a daily basis. How long have you been living in the city? Is this your first day?"

"I've been living in Manhattan for twenty-five years and change."

"Tell me about the windows wherever you live."

He had me there, but I wasn't inclined to say so. "Look, Mr. Abramovitz, I looked all over that room the way they've left it, and some things don't add up."

"They don't, huh? Sonny, the suicide note, the .38 with only Cutler's prints on it, the locked everything—all of it is, in first-grade math, two and two. Adds up to four. Always does. If there's anythin' about that suicide that stops me, it's why someone rich as Cutler was supposed to be, with all that money, would take himself out of the picture. But he's not the first, and he won't be the last.

"But I'll tell you what I'm gonna do. You got me riled up, so I'm gonna do something I've never done before on a case I closed in the time it takes to snuff out a cigarette butt. I'm going to come down there and show you there are things upstart detectives need to know. I assume good-ol' on-site Nosey Parker—whatever she calls herself—can still get us in. If she can't, which she shouldn't, I don't wanna deal with any real estate agent. Somebody's got to do their flea-bitten job. Just be glad it's not you or me. I know the buildin'. I remember every crime scene I ever spent time on. That's the kind of Fearless Fosdick I am."

I got his riling loud and clear.

"I'd like to say I'm gonna drop everythin' and meet you right away. Not in the cards. I thought when I took retirement, which I'm not going to go into with the likes of you, I'd have plenty time to myself. Wrong. Not when you have the kind of family I have. Hardly a one of 'em who still don't ask me to get rid of a parking ticket and worse. There's the door now." In the background I heard the kind of buzzer that could wake the dead. "Another *shnorrer*. The best I can do is say meet me in front of that building tomorrow. I'm not in that much of a hurry for this wild goose chase. So let's say noon. On the dot. If I run into any trouble, you'd better give me your number."

I obliged. Without saying any more, let alone wait for me to say any more, he rang off. I had the impression he didn't think anything additional I might offer would be of any interest to him. He'd already written me off and would eminently finalize that as rapidly as he could after noon the next day.

I'll show him, I said alone, as if I were declaring my certainty to him. But the "I'll show him" was as much to convince myself as it was to knock him off his former detective sergeant high horse.

It was late morning, and I remained caught up with this new escapade, too primed not to get to following my new nose for clues. I had some toast with jam and drank seltzer straight from the bottle. I wasn't inclined to fix something stronger, not because I wanted to keep my mind clear but because I never think of mixing myself a drink, certainly not so early in the day. Over the years the bottles in my liquor cabinet have all but collected cobwebs. If I were going to be a novice private eye, I wouldn't be from the guzzling variety.

While moving on to mac-and-cheese, I recalled Harold Swirner wondering how much I knew about Fulton Cutler. That struck me as worth pursuing. Had there been a *New York Times* obituary? If there had been, it was an obit commemorating somebody of whom I'd never heard and so wasn't likely to read. Harold Swirner couldn't have meant the *Dayton Daily News.* He'd undoubtedly never had enough interest in Fulton Cutler to arm himself with that much background.

I do admit that at forty-two I'd already become someone who often, if not always, starts reading the *Times* on the obituary page—not infrequently conceding it remains up in the air whether I'll ever appear there.

I cleared up the little I needed to clear up of my meager bachelor's brunch and went to the computer. I googled Fulton Cutler, found what I was looking for in the *Dayton*

Daily News. That wasn't too surprising, since all the obits I'd found in the man's scrapbook were from the *Dayton Daily News.* Although identifying Fulton Reginald Cutler as a "prominent financier," the obit, published within a month of Fulton Cutler's death, was on the skimpy side. It noted that "Cutler, 78, a venture capitalist known for his benevolence as well as his reclusiveness," had died in New York City several weeks earlier, no cause of death given. Included were his graduation from St. Paul's Preparatory Academy and Harvard. His Dayton birth was noted as were his parents, Reginald Thomas Cutler and Hyacinth Lois Reardon Cutler, and his membership in The Fifth Street Fraternity, "a local aggregate of private pursuits." Mr. Cutler, it said, had never married, that there were no survivors and that "the will is to be read at a later date."

Odd for a man of means, I thought, but no explanation was going to come to me from the primary source. I thought about the no-cause-of-death statement. Had someone prevailed over not revealing the "suicide," or was the obit written in part from a discreet coroner's report?

Is there such a thing? I looked it up. The rules are vague and can be affected by, for instance, a family request. Was a Cutler family member involved? Did I need to find out? Izzy Abramovitz might know. I'd ask him.

Ask him when I saw him, which, if my math worked

out, wasn't for another twenty hours, give or take. In the interim, I knew how I ought to spend the time. I'd interview individually as many of Ms. Belfer's cohorts as I could round up.

I made a list according to Ms. Belfer's rundown. If I had it right—I think I did—the only qualifiers in the vicinity were No-First-Name Winger, dance instructor Amy Pritchard and cabbie Ed Snow, from whom I'd already extracted nothing anywhere near incriminating.

Doing what any curious person would do, I googled all three, Ed Snow just to be complete. To no avail. A few Amy Pritchards came up and maybe just as many Ed, or Edward, Snows. They were either dead—some as long dead as a hundred years and more—or still extant but nowhere near New York City. Too many Wingers to make any headway without a first and, even more helpful, middle name.

Those who'd occupied the building at the time of the murder but had since cleared out I'd have to locate later, if that were possible. There were dwellers in three of the previously inhabited apartments—those apartments now belonging to the Hilliards, Donny Prager, the trainer, and Jason Arnold, the painter.

I'd talked to Ed Snow and likely wouldn't get more from him. Or would I? Something Izzy Abramovitz said on the phone, almost as a throwaway, flagged me. "Rich as he was," he'd said. "With all that money," he'd said.

I thought about how often money had come up in the discussions I'd had so far. I thought about the police procedurals I'd read, how they're always harping on motive. I'd best keep money as motive uppermost in mind.

Money, motive.

Motive, money.

That's it. That's the definite ticket.

Maybe there was some incident Ed Snow hadn't brought up. He didn't like the deceased, but was Fulton Cutler's taking him in as "not much" sufficient motive for murder if money was somehow involved? Maybe it was in extreme circumstances. What about Amy Pritchard? What about No-First-Name Winger?

Time to talk to that perhaps money-hungry trio, any one of the three who might have been rapacious enough to rig a locked-room murder. That, of course, would depend on their somehow having finagled themselves into Fulton Cutler's will. How any one of them could have achieved that, I'd have to figure out later.

My plan was to sit on my stoop and when, and if, I sighted Pritchard or Winger, hurry to waylay them. There was a small detriment. Ms. Belfer. No question she'd be on her regular lookout, although she, of course, knew who they were. No, wait. She said No-First-Name Winger rode a fold-up bicycle. Amy Pritchard probably looked and dressed like someone who worked at a dance studio.

It was around one in the afternoon when I took my post, eyes peeled, ears cocked. At shortly after 1:30 by my cell phone Ms. Belfer hadn't arrived to stand guard, but No-First-Name Winger appeared. He was carrying a folded bike.

Down the stoop he came, a man about five foot seven with the kind of face that made him look like an aging teenager rather than a mature man. He wore a light cropped jacket with iridescent stripes, khaki trousers with a clasp on one ankle, running shoes and an orange helmet like a winged Mercury. When he reached the pavement, looking neither right nor left, he began to unfold the— wouldn't you know?—orange-framed bike.

This gave me ample time to take out the pad I was using as a prop and approach him. I introduced myself and explained my purpose, by now the old reliable writing-a-book-about-unsolved-New-York-City-murders. Continuing to complete the bike unfolding, he didn't look up. I let him finish the task. When he did, he looked at me, pointedly annoyed.

"Look, Mister—," he said in a smooth voice. "I forgot your name, but I have nothing to say to you. I don't know about any murders in this building. There was a suicide sometime back. At the time I told the cops everything I knew, which was nothing." He glared at me, as one of the ubiquitous meddlers.

I suppose that in my current capacity I was indeed one of the loathsome cohort but said, "Would you be interested in the subject if I told you that the suicide you think you knew about was actually a murder, Mister—uh, I don't know your name?"

He squinted at me, as if he wanted to bring me into clearer focus. "Not that it's any business of yours, it's Winger."

"You must have a first name."

He said brusquely, "John, if you have to know."

I waved my pad at him. "For my book."

"You'd be doing me a favor to leave me out of any specious book you're writing about a specious murder."

I said, "When I've finished my inquiries, the murder will be anything but specious." I tried to sound assured, although I wasn't yet one hundred percent certain. "If you don't mind, I would be grateful if you'd answer a very few questions."

"I do mind," John Winger said, his only slightly wrinkled aging teenage face reddening. "I told the police when they were investigating."

"When the police were investigating," I started, "they were investigating a suicide. Had they been investigating a murder, they might have asked different questions. For instance, they might have asked whether you or anyone let anyone into the building that night."

"I didn't," John Winger replied with a huff. "I almost never have any reason to let anyone into the building. I live alone, and I don't have many guests."

"And you saw no one leave."

"No."

He lived in the front of the building and so couldn't have seen anyone in the garden. Ed Snow and Amy Pritchard had those vantage points. I said, warily, "Fulton Cutler was a rich man."

"Hold it right there," John Winger leapt in. "Are you trying to ask me if I murdered Cutler for his money?"

"I didn't say that."

"You were just about to. I beat you to it. Here's what I know about him and his money. I never saw him much in the time I was living here and he was, too. But he looked like the kind of rich businessman so sold on himself that owning a gun, a revolver for protection wasn't something he needed. Maybe a lot of successful businessmen do, but he didn't."

John Winger pointed at his now locked-in-place bike, while the occasional passerby angled around us, and cars sailed up the street. "The only time I ever spoke to him was about my bike. My Brompton. I didn't have it then. He's the reason I have it now."

"The Brompton," I said, matter of factly. "Is that spelled as it sounds."

"B-r-o-m-p-t-o-n."

I wrote it down carefully and appended, just as matter of factly, "And he's the reason you have it."

"One day four or five years ago now, before he took his life or whatever, I was coming in with my bike—a Vilano E2, not the most expensive bike on the market but expensive enough—when he was coming out of his door. I was headed toward the stairs and was blocking him. Just for two seconds at the most, you understand. That didn't stop him from being aggravated.

"'Must you bring that thing into the building all the time?' he said. What did he think I was going to do, leave it out on the street to get stolen in half a minute, no matter how strong the lock you use? He said he was tired of watching me blocking his way. When he ever saw me blocking his way other than this one time, I'd like to know. I said, 'I bring it in because it's the only way I can keep it safe.' He said, 'And you don't mind getting in other people's way?' I said I rarely did—do—and he said, 'Can't you remove the wheels or fold it up somehow?'

"I said, 'I can't do that.' I threw in that there are bikes that can be folded, but I don't have that kind of money. Then he did the damndest thing. He said, 'What do they cost?' I said a Brompton—which is what I wanted to buy for years but couldn't—might cost as much as fifteen hundred dollars and more. 'Is that right?' he said and then, 'Wait here a minute.' He went back in his place and came back in no more than a minute and handed me a check for two thousand dollars. 'Take this,' he said, 'and don't let me catch you ever blocking my door again. I won't like it.'

"I looked at the check and was about to tell him I couldn't accept it and that anyway two thousand dollars was too much and to thank him for the offer, but he was too busy snarling. He wasn't waiting for a thank-you, anyway. He just put the check in my hand, pushed me out of the way and left. I figured I might as well cash the check, get the damn bike and give him a check with the leftover money. Which I did. I shoved it under his door.

"And here's the thing. He never cashed it. I guess he had money to throw away. I didn't see him much after that, and when I did, he'd look at me as if he'd never seen me before, the bastard. One of the only things I ever knew about him was he was some kind of investor."

I'd written some of this down, but after a while I stopped. John Winger's Truman-Capote-with-a-grudge look only got redder with occasional widening of his brown eyes. I thought you probably don't murder someone who's made it possible to buy you the bike of your dreams. And doesn't even cash a check for the excess dough.

Then again, it might have occurred to John Winger that if a man like Fulton Cutler is so casual about money that he doesn't bother to cash checks, he might be the source of even much more of it.

Then again, if Fulton Cutler looked through John Winger regularly with no seeming recognition after the Brompton exchange, it wasn't likely the latter would be getting anything further from the former.

Like Ed Snow, John Winger just provided his own dismissal from suspicion. Since he had no access to Fulton Cutler from the building's rear, that also dispatched him, as far as I was concerned just then.

Finishing up, John Winger shook his head sharply. It was as if he'd caught himself doing something he hadn't intended doing. "If you don't mind, I have to get going." He threw a leg over the bike and mounted it with aplomb.

"Of course, you do," I said. "I just have one more question." He began to object, but I carried on. "You didn't hear anything the night Fulton Cutler died?"

"I told the cops I didn't. Why would I tell you anything different? I never heard a thing. Once I go to sleep, I'm dead to the world."

I can't say what got into me, but I countered with, "So was Fulton Cutler. That night."

That was too much for John Winger. He looked at me with disgust, said nothing and pedaled off so quickly he all but cannonaded his Brompton and him off the curb into the street.

Next? Amy Pritchard? I wasn't about to find out immediately. I considered ringing her buzzer. Even Private Detection 101 would likely have suggested that as advisable, but it seemed to me that buzzer-ringing was a mite too proactive. I'd have to explain on the intercom who I was and what I was after.

I preferred catching Amy Pritchard slightly more off guard when she had no time—as with Ed Snow and John Winger—to frame any responses or, worse, refuse to talk to me at all, using the shopworn excuse that she had told the police everything she knew.

It was Ms. Belfer who resolved the minor predicament. While I was trying to conjure options, she materialized, resplendent in flannel. What I resorted to did take some snazzy finagling. And some fessing up. If I intended to wait for Amy Pritchard after John Winger had so conveniently accommodated me, I reckoned I couldn't sit on my stoop.

It could and probably would look fishy to looking-fishy maven Ms. Belfer. I suppose I could have sat on her stoop but that would have obligated me to talk to her whenever she was there. I was prepared to avoid that eventuality more than any number of viruses to which I might have been exposed over the years.

I decided my only recourse was to come clean. I told

Ms. Belfer I was waiting for Amy Pritchard but that I wasn't going to take up her, Ms. Belfer's, time as well. I said that my working on a book about unsolved New York City murders was drummed up.

"I knew there was something fishy about that," Ms. Belfer said, pretty much predictably.

I said I was only interested in the murder in her building, that I'd gotten faint wind of it from word on the block. In one regard that was true. I said I came to its attention because I live on the block, only a few buildings away. I said I was surprised we hadn't run into each other before. I didn't go so far as to vouch that the word I'd heard on the block—a host of words—was couched in the used 1953 *Great Gatsby* paperback she'd put out.

When I admitted all that, Ms. Belfer said she thought I'd looked familiar but that she couldn't place me. I replied that when I first saw her, she had looked familiar to me, too. I said perhaps that was because I haven't had the opportunity to populate my stoop as much as she had time to command hers.

I went on to reemphasize that getting in touch with any current tenant or co-op owner present and past was on my agenda, that, as she'd informed me, Amy Pritchard, John Winger and Ed Snow were the last of the current tenants holding over from the past. I said I'd already talked to the last two.

Other than having spouted her opinion about my original appearance on the stoop as fishy, she took my outpouring in stride. Then she added an especially useful tip. With almost anyone else in the building, she'd suggest ringing the buzzer. But she said that might not be productive with Amy Pritchard. She said she was familiar with Amy Pritchard's comings and goings—I had no reason to disbelieve her, did I?—and that on weekdays Amy Pritchard left the building at eleven in the morning and sometimes didn't return until "all hours."

"God knows what she's up to, but you can set your watch by eleven in the a.m.," Ms. Belfer said. "I can count on the fingers of one hand the times she varied from that schedule. So if you're smart, you'll go about your business—whatever that is—until then."

Not cottoning to sitting on her stoop for the next eighteen hours or whatever, I decided there were certain things about which Ms. Belfer could be trusted. This was one of them. I'd take the chance that today would not be the day Amy Pritchard changed her routine.

I went home where there were detection-related things I could be doing, such as finding the location of tenants who lived in the building when Fulton Cutler was helped to shuffle off his mortal coil, such as locating the tenants and/or co-op owners who had moved out and on.

How was I going to go about that? No detection

instincts snapped into place. I sat in the reading chair drumming my fingers and tapping my unshod right foot. While doing that, I sensed movement from the end table. *The Great Gatsby* appeared to be exhibiting its version of finger-drumming and toe-tapping.

I looked at the insolent thing. "Okay, all right," I wheezed at it. "I'd be doing something if I had any idea what." I was wracking my brain—or would have been if I knew how you actually wrack a brain. Does anyone?

Oh, hold it, hold it. Maybe I could get in touch with some of those Fifth Street Fraternity scions. But at this hour? I'd sat there, futilely ruminating so long it had gotten past ten.

I remained sitting, lost in a clue vortex, waiting for a revelation and getting none. It came to me that I was thunk out. The thing to do was rest. If the murder had sat unsolved for this long, another few hours wouldn't hurt solution prospects, protesting *Great Gatsby* volume or no protesting *Great Gatsby* volume.

THURSDAY

I slept late, not because I intended to. My dreams were chock-full of elusive premonitions and omens, tantalizing clarifications, but look what happens to Tantalus over and over and over: no satisfaction.

All the same, at 10:45, I was on my stoop. Ms. Belfer was on hers. At 11:00, or no more than a minute after, a woman about five foot two came out of the surveilled door. I wondered if she had eyes of blue. That was only a fleeting thought. Across the divide, Ms. Belfer gave me a raised eyebrow conspiratorial look that silently signaled, "She's who you think she is."

As Amy Pritchard all but pogoed down the stoop in a ruffled mini-skirted, fire-engine-red dress, I saw she was skittering toward Eighth Avenue. I'd have to hurry if I was going to catch her before she got to the corner. I did hurry but wasn't fast enough. She reached the corner and had gotten past the bike lane. Lucky for me, she'd stopped to hail a cab.

Not a one was heading in Amy Pritchard's direction, but she seemed to be remaining calm. Another stroke of luck as I approached. "Excuse me," I said. "I don't mean to bother you, but I hope you wouldn't mind if I asked you a few questions."

She looked at me with her come-hither blue eyes and said, "Why do people say they don't mean to bother you when they do mean to bother you? Don't answer that. As you can see, I'm trying to get a cab. When you don't need one, they're all over the place. When you do..." She let the sentence fade out and said, "What do you want to know? And I should tell you I'm very good at handling mashers. It's part of my professional training." She folded her right hand into a small fist and positioned herself more steadily on her feet in their low-heeled, fire-engine-red pumps.

"It's nothing like that," I said.

"It isn't? Then what's it like?"

"I saw you come out of your building, and it so happens it's a building I'm interested in."

"I've heard a lot of pick-up lines in my time, but this is a new one." She looked down the avenue cabward again but spotted nothing.

I said, "Trust me. This isn't a pick-up line."

"Trust me usually means, you better not trust me. That's another thing I know a lot about."

"I'm interested in your building because of a death that occurred there a while ago."

That seemed to mollify her. "Really," she said. "I don't know about any deaths in my building. We're all pretty healthy. There's a lot wrong with some of them in other ways, but I won't go into that. They can defend themselves."

"I'm talking about someone who died three years ago or so. Fulton Cutler."

"Oh, him, the guy who took his life. What about him? From what I know about him he was probably right to do it."

"I'm interested because I don't believe he did take his life. I think he was murdered."

Hearing my carefully measured statement, Amy Pritchard lost all interest in flagging cabs. "I don't know where you got that idea." She looked me up and down as if I might have escaped from an asylum. I was getting used to the look. "It was a suicide. The cops figured that out in two seconds flat. They interviewed all of us in the building at the time. I hope you haven't gotten it in your head that I'm one of the suspects. I'll tell you flat out I didn't like the guy. I told the cops. If he did himself in, he probably did the right thing."

She stopped to gauge how well I'd gotten her heated comments. I said, "I'm a writer and I'm writing a book about unsolved murders in New York City." For lack of anything better I trotted that one out again.

She thought it over and said, "What? A kind of *Naked City* about murders? So, okay, like, if he was murdered, he probably deserved it, but I didn't do it. Why would I?"

Now, Amy Pritchard forgot cabs entirely as well as any traffic kerfuffle, the overlapping whoosh of automobiles scrambling to outrun the lights. She pointed at a bench on the median. We sat. She put the hefty carryall she was carrying on her lap. Her mini-skirted dress was pulled up thigh high, verifying there was nothing amiss about her thighs and the rest of her legs.

"What I do is I'm a dance instructor. I work at a dance studio. No names, if you don't mind. I like it there, and they like me. I've been there twelve years now, but I don't just work at the studio. I give private lessons. Not too long after I moved into my building—the one you're so interested in—I was going to work, and that man...I never remember his name. Collins? Cummings?"

"Fulton Cutler."

"Yeah. That man was coming in. He had to step aside, 'cause I was already halfway out the inside door. He didn't look happy about it. I figured he was a neighbor, probably the first-floor neighbor I'd heard about from Ms. Belfer. By the way, that's part of why Cummings wasn't murdered. She would have seen any stranger coming in or leaving."

I picked her up on that. "At somewhere between one and four in the morning?"

"Okay, maybe not. Anyway, shortly after I moved in, I'm going in and Collins is coming out. I figure I'll be nice and introduce myself. I start to say hello, and he only looks at me like I'm a piece of lint on his lapel. I say I'm a neighbor upstairs, Amy Pritchard. I'm a dance teacher. I expect he'll say his name. Most people would, but he doesn't. I already stuck my hand out and am waiting for him to shake. Don't tell me. I know. A woman is supposed to wait for a man to put his hand out first. Or is it the other way around?

"Anyways, he looks at my hand as if it's about to bite him and steps right around me. I think, Get him, Mister High and Mighty, and started to go on my way. But I don't even get the outer door completely open when I hear, 'Excuse me, young woman.' I told him my name not two minutes ago and already he doesn't remember it. 'Did you say you give dance lessons?' So I stop and turn around. He's holding the inner door open. 'Yeah, I give dance lessons. What about it?' I was in no mood to be friendly after the way he treated me up to then."

I wondered if I could see where this back and forth was going. I thought I did. I suppose anyone might.

She said, "Well, don't you know he says, he wonders if I give private lessons. I wasn't sure I wanted to give any private lessons to this old geezer. Not that old geezers aren't a big part of my clientele. I always need the money. A single girl has to fend for herself in the big city. That's no big news flash."

No, I thought, that's no big news flash.

"I say I do give private lessons, and he says, 'I could use some,' or something along those lines. I figure I better tie him down. I talk times with him and give him my rates. And there's, like, the added plus he's in the building. I don't even have to worry about carfare."

A money concern? Hmm.

She carries on. "I tell him my freest times are later in the evenings because most days I'm at the studio until eight or thereabouts. So we fix an appointment for three days later. It's always a good idea to keep them waiting."

My guess is that as she spoke, Amy Pritchard knew she was attracting attention. She knew the power of her body. So, evidently, did Fulton Cutler, if what she'd said about him was any indication. But was it the body of a murderer?

Whether or not, Amy Pritchard had dropped the smile. "Anyways, the night comes. When we get to that back room of his—where he shot himself or somebody else did; I couldn't care less which—he doesn't want to do any of the dances in my repertoire. Let's just say we got into the basics of the Foxtrot, and when I move on to showing him how to dip, he thinks that's an invitation to do something else. Which is not, like, a dance step. I don't put up with that. I push him off or try to, but he holds on to me.

"I'm struggling and he's struggling, and I get the

feeling I know where he's heading. But I've got a strong knee and use it. He lets go, and I'm out of there like a shot. Whoops. Wrong word. I don't wait for him to pay me. I don't care how rich he is or who he thinks he is. The guy tried to—. You know what he tried to do. And I'm not going to forget that so fast."

Oh, she isn't? I'm thinking. If she's not forgetting so fast, what's she going to do about it? Do I have a live one here? Was she angry enough that she did something about it?

I'd keep that in mind. I said, trying to seem as if I were just taking it all in equably. "I can see where you wouldn't forget so fast," I said. "Who would? Well, Ms. Pritchard, you've been a big help in my research." I closed my pad and stood up. "Thanks so much for your time."

She lifted the carryall from her lap and stood up. She said, "You seem like a nice enough guy. If you ever want to take any dance lessons, let me know. You obviously know where to find me."

I did, and why all at once did the comment sound ominous? What might she be carrying in the bulging car-ryall? Did I see the outline of a pistol there, at the ready for overreaching Foxtrot wannabes? That's what I was asking myself, as she put her hand up to hail a cab and got one immediately.

I stayed where I was. I had a few things to think over.

Motives. Money. Could be that now there was another motive to consider, a motive stronger than money. But is there any motive stronger than money?

I was dwelling on my fledgling, possibly promising, last interrogation when I suddenly realized it was almost noon and therefore almost Izzy Abramovitz hour.

I was so fired up to cover the distance from the corner where I'd left Amy Pritchard—or she'd left me—with maybe, just maybe, something to go on that I couldn't get to the late Fulton Cutler's former building speedily enough.

I wasn't going to keep Izzy Abramovitz waiting. From the sound of him, he might not wait to arrive on the dot of noon or on a few dots before that.

He wasn't there yet—it was 11:56 by my watch—but Ms. Belfer was all turned out in a freshly laundered flannel bathrobe. Why so dressed up? Had she understood that something of neighborly import was about to transpire?

Whether or not, it was a promising break. I launched into my spiel about a police detective joining us at any moment, that my suspicion that a murder and not a suicide had taken place in Fulton Cutler's former and still unsold floor-through was about to be taken seriously by a genuine professional.

That was something of an exaggeration, but not so big

a one now that Amy Pritchard's testimony was still bubbling. Once I'd proved my conviction one way or another, it would undeniably be taken very seriously.

Looking skeptical—a look Ms. Belfer was a past mistress of—she asked, "Don't tell me they're reopening the case after all this time."

"I won't tell you that, Ms. Belfer. So far, the precinct is dragging its feet. It's not easy for an entire precinct to confront being wrong. Instead, I have someone who was on the case and has since retired meeting me here today."

"I wonder who that could be," Ms. Belfer said, scratching her head with the hand that wasn't tightly holding the recently laundered flannel bathrobe. "I hope it isn't that awful Abramovitz man. Tell me it's not him."

"I'm afraid I can't tell you that, Ms. Belfer."

"He's coming here? He's a horrible man. One of those couple of days he was going in and out of here, he had the nerve to call me a busybody. A busybody, when all I want is to do a good turn here and there. I won't be glad to let him into the building, but I told you I would help you, and I will. I don't go back on my word. Just don't expect me to be cordial to him, and I can be cordial when I want to be. I can be as cordial as the next one. Even more cordial."

Since Ms. Belfer and I were so engaged in this tetchy exchange, we hadn't seen the man under discussion arrive.

We heard him first. "If it ain't my old friend Ms. Belfer," he said in a gravel-stoked voice I recognized from our phone conversation.

Ms. Belfer, who without question leaves a lasting impression, issued a palpable harrumph. That's if a harrumph could be palpable. This one was.

Ignoring it, as I hoped Izzy Abramovitz was also doing, I turned and saw at the bottom of the stoop a man with one big worn-down wingtip-shod foot planted on the first step. He was just this side of obese. At roughly five foot eight, he carried himself as if he were six foot eight. The pate was bald. What hadn't balded was closely shaved. His face was round, a confederation of wrinkles embracing a bulbous nose. He had a fleshy mouth and a couple of chins. He was wearing a capacious brown suit that might have cost him as much as forty dollars a few decades back. His striped shirt had a collar from the same era as his suit.

I'm saving the eyes for last. Under eyebrows that needed a hedge trimmer to tame them, his eyes were dark, most likely black from my perspective. Piercing only begins to get them. Laser-like understates their effect. The eyes not only had it but played it to the max.

What they told me right off is that he wasn't here to play games. He wasn't here to have his judgment questioned. He wasn't here to have it reversed. He was here to overcome.

"And who's that with you, Ms. Belfer? I'm gonna guess it's buddin' private detective Daniel Freund. They'll all tell you my guesses don't go amiss."

My turn to speak, I said, "I'm Daniel Freund, Mister Abramovitz. Do I call you Mr. Abramovitz or Officer Abramovitz or Detective Sergeant Abramovitz? I don't know the protocol."

I was starting down the steps with my hand held out as Izzy Abramovitz said, "Oh, so you're one of the protocol boys. I had my fill of protocol right up to the day I retired. Now I don't have truck with any of that guff. You call me Izzy and like it."

He waited for me to come down to his level, and I mean that in more than one sense of the phrase. Or to understand that in his estimation my psychological status was a level definitely lower than his.

When I had taken all this in, at least in the physical realm, we shook hands. He had a small hand, but he used it as if it was the hand of, no surprise, someone six foot eight. It was as if we were entrants in a hand-wrestling competition. It was some grip. I tried to give back in kind but was only good enough to last until he relaxed his mitt.

He was letting me know he'd be in charge from here on out.

I could only think that I'd cede that much to him but not lose sight of the mission on which the 1953 *Great*

Gatsby edition had sent me. I also recalled that the grip of the hand urging me through F. Scott's masterwork was no less powerful than Izzy Abramovitz's.

When he took his hand back, he said, "Okay, boychik, you say you have somethin' to show me. So show me." Then he spoke to Ms. Belfer, "I don't imagine you'll be coming with us, will you, Ms. Belfer?"

Ms. Belfer didn't argue. She only said, "I will be gracious enough to get you into the building. Mister Freund will appreciate me for that. I've been his accomplice—."

"That's an innerestin' choice of words, Ms. Belfer," Izzy Abramovitz interrupted.

"I'm glad you recognize that, Officer Abramovitz. I always choose my words carefully, unlike some I could name."

Izzy Abramovitz paid no attention to that. He opted to poke me in the side and point up the stoop. Ms. Belfer, saying nothing, admitted us. Izzy Abramovitz thanked her. Looking slightly stricken, she held the inner door open.

Izzy Abramovitz said to her, "Aren't you going to let us into the Cutler apartment? I wouldn't put it past you to have keys." Ms. Belfer looked as if she wanted to respond to that but held off.

In a hurry, I said, "The door is open. Ms. Belfer is convinced the real estate agent forgets to lock it every time he leaves. She closes it but can't lock it. Lucky for us."

Okay, okay, I was prevaricating.

"Very lucky," Izzy Abramovitz said, making it plain he didn't believe a word of what I was saying. He'd seen and heard it all before.

I didn't want to linger on this. I opened the door and ushered us in. Before he entered, he gave me another of his penetrating glares. I figured I was in for a barrage of them but behaved as if I hadn't even caught the look.

I closed the door behind us, taking in one last glare from Ms. Belfer. I had no doubt she'd stay where she was until Izzy Abramovitz and I reappeared. She'd want to learn whatever we'd deign to tell her.

I knew I wouldn't divulge much. If anything. I suspected that if Izzy Abramovitz said something illuminating, it would be no more than a tease.

With no reason for inspecting the other rooms, he and I reached the Fulton Cutler study in seconds. He preceded me. He knew the way, of course. He walked through the open door, stood there and, when I entered, extended his short arm—the sleeves of his brown suit were a few inches too long.

"All right, smart guy Freund," he said, "show me where I went wrong." Then, looking more widely around the room, he said, "Hey, nothin' changed, or almost nothin'. What are they turnin' the place into? A suicide museum?" He aimed the black eyes at me. "Forgive me, Daniel Freund, I mean a murder museum. We're here to have you toss my conclusion into a cocked hat, whatever that is. I don't wear hats myself. What, to hide my bald head?" He patted it. "I'm bald. So what? You'd be surprised how many women think a bald head is sexy. They can't wait to pat it, rub it, kiss it. I let 'em."

He started walking around the room. He went to the left side of the desk and pointed at Fulton Cutler's chair. "He was slumped over on the desk. The blood had dried on his head and on the blotter. The coroner estimated he'd been dead for at least two days. Rigor and all that beeswax. That's how long it took for his cleanin' lady to come in and find the door locked, which she said had never been locked before when she was there. She saw him nowhere else, got suspicious and called the cops. She didn't know who else to call. Ms. Belfer, who thinks she sees everythin', said she saw nothin' strange but then shut her mouth for a change.

"When we got here and broke down the door—the locksmith was good for nothin'—and got to Cutler, deader than the Mets this season, his right arm was hangin' down. The .38 was there." He pointed at the floor. "There are those'll tell you he shoulda still been grippin' it. They'd be wrong. He'da lost all muscular control and dropped it.

"There are those'll tell you he couldn'ta shot himself.

He was left-handed. You one of them? That's as much as you or they know. He was right-handed. We verified that. You only had to look at the callus on his right index finger.

"What more do you need to know? We were handed the only deduction you could draw on a silver platter. Like I told you on the phone, I only wish all the cases I handled were as simple as this one."

I remembered something. Innocent as a baby lamb, I said, "When I talked to you on the phone, you said you were handling other cases at the same time you were investigating this one."

"Look here, boy-o, what are you askin'? If I rushed this one under pressure? That's not how I work."

"I didn't mean anything like that," I said, meaning exactly that. "I was just wondering."

"Keep the wonderin' to yourself. I'm more innerested in what you think you turned up here."

"Okay. When I was shown around the room—."

"By the agent?"

"Yes."

"Were you looking to buy this place? Izzy asked and smirked. "Forgive me, but you don't look like the buyin' type."

How was I to answer that? I didn't think my writing-a-book-on-unsolved-New-York-City-murders would fly.

I might have said I wanted to see what a place I might someday be able to buy would look like. I decided to be honest. More or less, mostly less. "I got wind that there had been a murder here that had been declared a suicide. I wanted to check it out."

"Wheredya hear that?"

"Just around. You know. You hear things."

"You do, do ya? I'd like to know where."

I wasn't about to tell him the 1953 *Great Gatsby* paperback edition. "Oh, you know, around. I forget exactly where."

The black eyes high-beamed again and then, "Okay, I'm not gonna press you. For now. Just tell me how I got it all wrong."

"Well," I began, "I'm not saying you got it all wrong."

"You're not? Don't soft-soap me, Mister Freund. That's exackly what you're sayin'. Get to it."

I got to it. Or thought I would. There was so much I had to say I didn't know where to start. Besides that, Izzy Abramovitz of the flinchless black eyes had me so flustered I wasn't certain I'd remember any of it.

Coming around, I silently whispered to myself, this is the Izzy Abramovitz technique, don't give in to it. Perhaps many others had, maybe even others on the Fulton Cutler case who differed with him in any way—e.g., the "half-wit" Patrick Dugan. I'll meet him at his level, and I didn't mean the five-foot-seven level but the six-foot-eight level to which he'd raised himself.

Bracing myself, I went directly to the desk, where the stager had decided to show what a working study could look like.

"There are a couple of things here I'm not certain I buy."

"Izzat so, and what would they be?"

"Not that the so-called suicide note isn't here. I assumed that was kept as evidence."

"So you're giving the precinct credit for somethin'."

"Yes, but I also figure a suicide note wouldn't be too enticing for prospective buyers to see."

"So far, Mister Freund, I have to give your private detecting high marks."

No need to go into the heavy dose of sarcasm that swaddled the Izzy Abramovitz comment.

"I do question the *New York Times* being here."

"No question, Mister Freund, you're batting a thousand," he said, approaching the table. "the *New York Times* wasn't there. It was an out-of-town paper."

"Yes, but what out-of-town paper?" I asked, allowing a speck of acid into the query.

"Didn't matter. Lots of people read out-of-town papers. When you have a door locked that we had to force open, when the windows are locked, when the Magnum

.38 is inches from the deceased's hand, when the suicide note on the dead man's stationery says, "I've had enough of this" and is starin' at you like a hooker on Forty-second Street—when there were still hookers on Forty-second Street—you don't have to use up too many brain cells. Even an upstart like you could solve the—uh—mystery."

Izzy Abramovitz was beginning to get my admittedly easily gettable goat. "But, Izzy," I said, "this is one upstart who's doubting the solved mystery."

"Awright, awright. Go on. You're takin' up my valuable time."

I wondered how valuable his time was at this point in his retirement, if what he mostly had to do was cater to, as he'd said on the phone, *shnorrers* of his acquaintance.

Not about to chase that line of thought, which Izzy Abramovitz would have had reason to find insulting (I would have, had it been aimed at me), I went back to the discussion at hand. I said, "Let's put aside whatever the right newspaper would be for the moment and take a look at the scrapbook alongside it. Which I assume it was when you started investigating."

"It was. What about it? It was closed, like it is now. I—we—figured Cutler was going to cut somethin' out of the paper and put it in the scrapbook, but he didn't get around to that before he sent himself to the pearly gates or wherever he was bound. So why examine the scrapbook? I might have flipped through it to see if Cutler had written anything else in there about having enough, but there was nothing like that in or on the pages I eyeballed."

"You didn't notice everything he'd pasted there were obituaries."

More Izzy sourness. "Where are you goin' with all this?"

"I'm going back to the out-of-town newspaper, which I believe was the *Dayton Daily News*. Dayton, Ohio."

"I know where Dayton is."

"That's the thing about it, Izzy." He was looking at me as if he regretted he'd told me to call him Izzy. "All the obituaries in the scrapbook are from the *Dayton Daily News*. Why would that be if he wasn't from Dayton? I looked up an obituary for Fulton Cutler in the *Dayton Daily News,* and there he was."

"Bully for the *Dayton Daily News*. They ran an obit for one of their own. I bet you a buck they do that pretty much every day. You don't have me shoutin' murder yet. Anythin' else, sonny boy? I do notice somethin' different you ain't brought up."

This was news. Was he about to come over to my side?

He wasn't. Instead, he said, "The blotter thing. You know, the leather mat all these things are on. It's different. They replaced it. Guess they had to. Like I said, the one here then had blood on it. You know, boy-o, from the gunshot. You can never tell about that. Anything can happen, but from the angle he shot himself—." No, he wasn't coming over to my side. "—he did it so the bullet lodged in his skull, as it can do, and only caused internal bleedin' and some minor bleedin' from the nose. Bye-bye, blotter. This one they replaced it with ain't as nice. Why spend the money?"

Curses, foiled again. "What about the windows?" I said, changing the subject in a hurry and feeling as if I were grabbing at straws when I was convinced I wasn't. Was I becoming less convinced? I repeated, "What about them?" I beckoned him to follow me. He'd been grilling me from the other side of the desk. "They're both shut."

"I know that." He went from window to window. "They were then. They are now. What about 'em? Nobody's done anythin' about 'em. Brokers probably don't worry about buyers checkin' to see if windows open and close."

"The one you're standing by," I said, "is locked in place. The latch is shot, but this one—" I pointed to the place where a latch should have been. Izzy Abramovitz joined me. "—isn't locked, and still the window doesn't budge."

Again, I attempted to raise the lower frame. I couldn't. Neither could Izzy Abramovitz, whose elbow grease supply bettered mine.

He said, "If this is the first time you couldn't get a window to budge in New York City, you're the only one. It doesn't take a detective to tell you old buildins like this one are always settlin'. That's what happened here. Or somethin' like it. They're probably lucky they can open their doors. Maybe I should get Ms. Belfer in here. She could probably tell you about every door and window in the buildin' that won't open. Or won't stay shut. I don't think you're onto anything there."

Was he right about that? I was beginning to think he might be. I looked at the desk again and saw the Flex Seal standing with the other items, the scissors that hadn't been used to clip a latest obituary from the *Dayton Daily News* edition that, no question, must have attracted Fulton Cutler's notice.

I was determined to be determined. Or act as if I were. "All right, say Fulton Cutler shot himself."

"I've said it all along. I said it three years ago. I still say it."

I repeated myself. "But imagine he did. He got out all the things he needed to put his latest obit into his scrap-book. Why would he do all that and then shoot himself before he finished what he started?"

"Because, boychik, that's not what he started out to do. What he started out to do was shoot himself. And that's what he did." He stopped for a moment, took on an expression I hadn't seen before. His aging face was even reflective. That's if Izzy Abramovitz ever did anything close to reflecting.

He said, "But that open Flex Seal tub. That's a funny thing. When we came into the room and started logging things, the Flex Seal tub wasn't on the desk. It probably had been, but when we came in, it was on the floor between the weapon and the window. Stands to reason whoever staged the room put it on the desk with the other scrapbook items."

That reminded me. "If they'd gone through the desk drawers, they might have found a bottle of Elmer's Glue-All. Why would Fulton Cutler have both?"

Why hadn't I thought of that until now?

Izzy Abramovitz didn't take much time to think about that. "Why does anyone have two of anythin'? Does it fly in the face of customer loyalty? Not these days. The lady who cleans my place can't decide between Clorox and Lysol. She leaves me notes. I can't keep 'em straight."

He started backing toward the door. "Look, Daniel Freund, in the past cotton-pickin' half-hour you showed me several things. So far, nothing convinces me I got the case wrong. I'm surer of it than I ever was. So, okay, this has been a nice experience. I've got you to thank for that. Now why don't we get the hell out of here?" He was backing out of the study door, which we had left open.

I followed him on his way to the stoop. Aside from a few guttural expulsions, he didn't say anything until we got to and through the outer door. Then he said, with sarcasm icicles instantly forming in the air, "Enjoy the rest of your day, Ms. Belfer."

At the bottom of the stoop, he shook my hand and said, "Boychik, for some reason you think you're on to somethin'. You're on to nothin'. Why keep wastin' your time? You already wasted too much of mine." He put out his hand, I shook it, enduring the pain close-mouthed. He added, "Thanks for nothin', and if by any stubborn chance you think you come up with somethin' else, leave me out of it. You got that? Leave me out of it. You got my number. I got yours. Let's both tear 'em up."

Not another word, as he trundled on his heavy feet to Eighth Avenue, leaving me high and dry. He was the expert here, after all—such an experienced expert that I had practically cowered to him.

And I hadn't even thought to throw Amy Pritchard into the mix. But where would that have gotten me when he was wedded to the open-and-shut case at the same time a woman possibly packing a pistol in her carryall was running—and dancing the Foxtrot—around free?

On that sour note, I heard another one. Ms. Belfer was saying, "Why did you have to bring that old crank around here, anyway?"

I looked up at her and replied, not without a meager drop of venom, "You got me there, Ms. Belfer" and walked away on my flatfoot's flat feet.

What to do next? Go home and think. I couldn't write off Izzy Abramovitz. He'd written me off.

I climbed my stairs like a man with no future. I opened the door and closed it behind me. I sat down in my reading chair. "I give up," I said to the empty room.

"No, you don't," the empty room said to me.

Only it wasn't empty. Siegel 1953 could speak. In its way. Lying flat, it started to move back and forth, as if furiously shaking its head.

Losing my temper with it again, I said, "You're not going to stop any of this carrying on, are you? What if I said dancing instructor Amy Pritchard?"

The goddam edition stopped shifting back and forth, rose into the air at least two inches and slammed flat down with an impassioned thud and the other-worldly sound of what I took to be *Great Gatsby* backup singers, perhaps the rowdy crowd that joined Daisy and Tom at the Plaza.

The animated inanimate object knew what it wanted. I took its unprecedented paroxysm to mean it had been in Fulton Cutler's study when the murder was committed. Was it dismissing Amy Pritchard? Was it fingering her, as only this 1953 copy could? It knew more even than Izzy Abramovitz.

Izzy Abramovitz wasn't there, was he?

I sat upright with renewed purpose. All right, I sat upright with partially renewed purpose. If the evidence I hoped I could show Izzy Abramovitz was insufficient, I'd better come up with more convincing evidence—and not anything about Amy Pritchard. Not that, by Izzy Abramovitz's parting declaration, I'd be showing him anything.

The thing to do right then, I reckoned, looking at the large vintage clock on the living room wall—2:03—was to determine the whereabouts for the three circa Fulton Cutler occupants who'd moved on from the building. They may surface with no discernible money motive either, or any other motive, but hadn't I repeatedly heard and read that in cases like Fulton Cutler's everyone is a suspect until proven otherwise. To my way of thinking, Amy Pritchard remained one. Could be, others could, too.

I flashed back on Ms. Belfer's renters and co-opers rundown. Her peroration seemed remarkably thorough at the time, but I realized she hadn't included any contact information on three former occupants, nothing for the chef Raoul Paget, nothing for the background-less C. F. Congdon, nothing for the mysterious, as she'd clocked him, night owl George Reiser. One was whoever lived in the garden apartment. Ms. Belfer had specified that was C. F. Congdon. The others were lodged upstairs.

I pondered them over a grilled cheese sandwich. I had their names. I'm living in the modern world. Something occurred to me that should have already occurred to me. There are a million ways to locate people, if, that is, they're still living.

Time to get right on it, and here's where Google came in, as did LinkedIn. For Raoul Paget, anyway. Google turned up three Raoul Pagets—some names aren't as obscure as you might suppose—but details narrowed them down to one, a San Francisco chef with a listed phone number.

This Raoul Paget was the only one who'd manned a Manhattan kitchen before crossing from sea to shining sea to establish a San Francisco French-American fusion restaurant. The background account I found reported that Côte d'Azur threw wide its Bay-area doors no more than six months after Fulton Cutler bit the Chelsea, Manhattan, dust.

If money is the traditional murder motive, where did Paget get his for such an expensive undertaking? An interview in the *San Francisco Chronicle* informed googlers that his backers had asked him to keep them anonymous. Was Fulton Cutler one? The *Chronicle* interviewer also pointed out that Paget had perfected Le Couteau, a kitchen knife he'd patented. Sounds like the perfect murder weapon, no? (It had to Ms. Belfer.) But the weapon in my impromptu investigation was a Magnum .38 lying near Fulton Cutler's right hand, not a designer knife in his back.

Moreover, if Raoul Paget had plotted a successful way to kill Fulton Cutler, how would he have managed to collect any (more?) money from the estate? He had no valid claim. Might he have thought he had? Might he have a different motive? Might he have thought he was somehow named in Fulton Cutler's will? Not likely, but I was obliged to check, wasn't I?

No time like the present. I did additional googling and found the Côte d'Azur phone number. I'd decided that was the subtler way in rather than using the listed number I had. I dialed it and was greeted with a masculine hello that sounded, unsurprisingly, like an "Allo." In the background, I heard the clinking and tinkling of crockery and utensils.

"May I help you?" the man asked.

I said, "You can, if you connect me to Raoul Paget."

"This is Raoul Paget." This took me aback. "Do you want to make a reservation?" This said with a still detectable Rah-ool Pah-jhay accent.

"I'm afraid not, Monsieur Paget. My name is Daniel Freund. I'm calling to ask about an incident in New York when you were still living here."

"You have called me during my busy lunch hour,"

Raoul Paget said, annoyance clouding his voice. "I have no time to speak to you about any Manhattan incident, whatever such an incident might be."

"It's about a man called Fulton Cutler," I said, trying to garnish *my* voice with mystery.

"Fooltone Cutlaire, Fooltone Cutlaire," Raoul Paget repeated. "I know no Fooltone Cutlaire—," he started to say, stopped himself and slowly said, "Oh, yes, I do know a man by that name—did know a man by that name. Give me your number, Monsieur Freund, and I'll try to return your call *immédiatement,* or if not *immédiatement, en bon temps.*"

I thought I picked up urgency from him, so did as he requested and hung up.

Having no idea how he interpreted *immédiatement,* I decided that rather than hasten on, I'd wait a few minutes but no longer for his call. I glanced at the end table to see if any complaints were simmering there.

Nothing but a cat-like purr. Jordan Baker's?

Before five minutes passed, my cell phone rang.

"Hello, Daniel Freund here."

A French-accented voice said, "Rah-ool Pah-jhay returning your call, Monsieur Freund." There was no background hubbub. He must have gone to an office for privacy. What might that portend? "You asked me about Fooltone Cutlaire, and, yes, I met once a man with that name. He lived in a *bâtiment* where I lived in Manhattan. I met him once. *Une fois seulement. Pas de politesse, cet homme.* We were leaving *cette maison* at the same time. I introduced myself and waited for heem to introduce heemself. *Finalement,* he said he was Fooltone Cutlaire. I repeated the name, but he corrected me. He said his name was Cutler, like Cutler-y but without the 'y.'

"At the time he said that, I was thinking about a name for a company I was starting for a new knife I was to market. I wanted to call it Rah-ool Pah-jhay *quelque chose ou autre. Immédiatement,* I thought Rah-ool Pah-jhay Cutlery. I said it out loud. He thought I was making the joke and walked away *vitement.* Now you call me. Le Couteau and my Côte D'Azur business are successful. You are looking for money, *probablement* for the word "cutlery." I know you Americans. I owe Monsieur Cutlaire nothing for using the word. I know he is—was— *un suicide*—but not I hope you think of me for that. Not for *un seul mot.* If you are *un avocat*—a lawyer—for his estate, I owe you nothing. *Rien. Pas un sou. Au revoir,* Monsieur Freund."

With the curt "au revoir," he rang off, not in any way sounding like a man who had sought Fulton Cutler's money or anything else.

I looked at the end table again: the same cat-like purr, only more pronounced. It told me I was in the right forest but barking up the wrong tree. Make that, meowing up the wrong tree.

All right, what about George Reiser? Ms. Belfer hadn't given him the best resumé—something about staying home days, only going out nights, something about heading west after he left the building.

Not much to go on, but I figured I'd google him all the same. Nothing to lose, right? Extremely right. Not only did I lose nothing, I gained a good deal. Google yielded several George Reisers, and among them: George Reiser Enterprises, general offices Madison Avenue, phone number and all, venture capitalist outfit, images of George Reiser.

The images didn't clarify anything. Ms. Belfer hadn't given me a physical description of George Reiser.

But this one was a local. I dialed. Two rings, and, believe it or don't, an actual person answered, a male voice saying, "George Reiser Enterprises, how may I help you?"

A voice offering help. "I'd like to speak to Mister Reiser, please."

"May I ask who's calling?" And such manners.

"My name is Daniel Freund."

"Does Mister Reiser know you, Mister Freund?"

"No, he doesn't, but I'm calling about a situation he does know about."

"He doesn't know you, but you say it's a situation he does know about. Let me see if he's in. If that's okay."

I said that was fine.

There was a short pause during which Vivaldi played. Then, "I'm afraid Mister Reiser is busy with a client at the moment, but I can put you through to his assistant. If that's okay."

I said it was, thinking I was going through all this bother to reach—possibly—someone who would likely not be the George Reiser I wanted to reach.

After listening to more Vivaldi for only three or four seconds, I heard another even smoother male voice say, "George Reiser's office."

Not wanting to waste any more time, I skipped directly and acceleratedly into my spiel, "I'm trying to reach a George Reiser who lived in Chelsea some years ago about a situation in that building. I understand he may be busy, but if you could ascertain whether he is that George Reiser—I suspect he isn't—I will not bother him again."

The smoothie responded, "I hesitate to interrupt Mister Reiser, but—." A slight pause. I took it to indicate the (suited? tie-wearing?) smoothie was calculating the advisability of alerting his boss. "—if that's all you need to know, I will interrupt him."

Vivaldi for closer to a minute.

And then, "You say your name is Daniel Freund, and

you want to know if I ever lived in Chelsea?" This was a different, less smooth voice. "I did, but I have no idea why you'd be at all interested. I certainly hope you were not given my name by someone who calls herself Ms. Belfer."

"Well, as a matter of—," was all I got to say.

He surged on. "Bats in the Belfry was how I knew her but not to her face. Although she deserved it. Fancied herself the building know-it-all, was always after me about what I did, where I spent my time. I played dumb, really dumb. I played duh-dumb with her. She bought it hook, line and sinker, the gullible old biddy. When I moved out, she had her usual gall to ask where I was moving. I told her I didn't know. I was just heading west. I was headed to this office, after working on my new venture from what I was calling home then." He stopped for a split second. "If she's behind this call, I have nothing to say."

"She is, and she isn't," I wedged in, taking in that his tone was preemptory.

"What's the 'she isn't' part?"

"Uh," I started.

"You'd best get to the point," he said.

I did. "I'm calling about a suicide that took place in the building."

"That old man who shot himself. I know about that. What about it?"

"You may remember it was declared an open-and-shut case."

"I remember. So what?"

"The case has been reopened. Evidence has come to light that there was no suicide. It's now believed Fulton Cutler was murdered."

"Fulton Cutler. That was his name. I forgot that. I even had some dealings with him. If you could call it that. The old buzzard. He used to noise it around some circles that he had money. I should say Bats in the Belfry noised it around, and I thought I'd give her the benefit of the doubt on that one. I was looking for capitalization for the business I was forming. I looked him up in the usual ways. I discovered he had money but not the kind I was looking for in an investor.

"I ruled him out without ever exchanging a word with him. I went out nights. Maybe he didn't. You'd be surprised how few businessmen understand that real deals are made at night. Now you know everything I have to say about him, except I'm sorry if he was murdered. Nobody deserves that. Now, goodbye, Mister Freund, and let me tell you if you call again, I'll consider it harassment and make things difficult for you. And Ms. Belfer. Which I know how to do."

He hung up peremptorily.

"Which he knew how to do," he'd said. What did he

mean by that? Was he another possibility? Couldn't be, could it? Was he implying he could put in a quick call to the guys with their index finger pressed against a nostril? Had he ever reached out in that direction? Had his interaction with Fulton Cutler transpired not exactly as he'd described it?

Maybe I mightn't cross his name off my mental list so fast, I cogitated, as I turned to C. F. Congdon. I looked at the end table. F. Scott Fitzgerald's 1953 finest was slightly levitating. It hadn't been while I was talking to George Reiser but now it looked as if it was doing pushups.

"Money motive motive money?" I mumbled.

More pushups.

That told me I better be doing some of my own: computer pushups. I wasn't so rapidly accommodated by the usual-suspect websites. Googling got me nowhere. LinkedIn got me nowhere. There is a Congdon plethora, which narrows things down, but narrowing things to C. Congdon is no help. Congdons whose given names begin with C pop up but far too many to track down one-two-three—Charles, Christopher, Clinton, Craig, Cary, Cory. Their inaccessibility is compounded by little, if no, indication of where they currently reside, if they are even currently residing this side of the grave.

This detection wall threw me back on Ms. Belfer. Not literally. She wasn't, I hoped, my last resort. I hadn't wanted to go to her, but I realized I'd better. I assumed no one else relatively close at hand would likely have the answer to any remaining ex-tenant questions—not Harold Swirner, not the building's other current occupants who hardly evinced any great interest in each other, let alone former residents.

Ms. Belfer's unflagging finagling might pay off on C. F. Congdon.

Checking the time at 5:16 and shrugging my shoulders in acquiescence, I went to my stoop to see if Ms. Belfer was on hers. She was. I started toward her, calling her name. She heard me. I'd come to know her ears were primed for anything.

I reached her stoop, and, without climbing its seven steps, said, "Ms. Belfer, I've been looking into things, and I realize you haven't told me much about one of the three other people living here when Fulton Cutler was murdered, the one you said was named C. F. Congdon."

I was feeling so desperate that I waxed disingenuous. "And here you are, so observant. What else, if anything more, did you know—do you know—about that one? You must have known at least a few things."

"You think I'm holding out on you? Well, I never!"

"I'm not saying that, Ms. Belfer. I'm just wondering if maybe a few other bits and pieces of information have slipped your mind."

"Nothing ever slips my mind if I don't want it to. I don't have that kind of mind. You may, but I don't." Then she seemed to relent, not a familiar attitude, I calculated, "Maybe I know more about C. F. Congdon, not that I had much time for him. Or him for me. It was as if he was trying to avoid me."

I thought of pooh-poohing the very notion but stopped short.

She didn't. "Since he was down there"—she pointed below—"he had no reason to use the stoop. So he hurried in and out like an animal into and out of his hole. He even looked like some kind of animal, all gray and furtive."

"You make him sound awful," I said, playing the sly flatterer.

"I make him sound no worse than he was. Once in a while, he would say hello as if to charm me. That may work with some people but not with me. I'm not so easily charmed. And anyway, he failed in the charm department. I haven't lived this long not to recognize a phony when I see one."

"What did he look like? How tall, that kind of thing?"

She gave this some visible thought, her mouth pursing. "I estimate over six feet, somewhere around there. A big guy. Kind of scary but not bad looking." She pondered strenuously. "You could say he had something athletic about him, like when he was a kid, he played sports.

That's what I mean when I say furtive animal. Charging in and out."

Getting this modestly enhanced description of C. F. Congdon, I tried to envision the Belfer-Congdon encounters from the Congdon side. Perhaps he was a fellow who realized that chatting up Ms. Belfer was opening himself to more building sociability than he desired. If I inhabited the below-stairs dwelling, I might have behaved exactly like Congdon.

Wanting to find out what I wanted to find out, I skipped to the moment's point. "Okay, I know that a Mr. Congdon lived here as C. F. Congdon. No first name given. For that matter, no middle name given. Do you happen to know what his first name was? Is?"

Ms. Belfer assumed one of her several self-satisfied expressions, many of them accompanied by folding her arms across her flannelled chest. "I certainly do and not from the C. F. Congdon name on the building directory and on his mailbox. The C. F. Congdon name wasn't on the directory or on the mailbox. Talk about hiding something. But I know how to take care of that. One day not long after he moved in downstairs, when he thought he was going to make a fast getaway, I decided to get him to fess up. I called over to him and said, as if butter wouldn't melt in my mouth, just like Scarlett O'Hara in *Gone With the Wind,* I said, 'You know, young man, you've been here a while, but I don't even know your name.' He garbled something. 'What's that, young man?' I said. 'You really need to speak up if you want anyone to pay attention to you.' That's when he said, 'C. F. Congdon.' He still garbled it. I said, 'What?' He repeated it. 'C. F. Congdon.' 'Mister Congdon,' I said, 'That's a nice name. You only use initials for your first and middle names? If we're going to be friends, as I hope we will be, I wonder if you'll tell me your name or names. I'll tell you mine.'"

I remembered that Ms. Belfer's name on the building directory was E. Belfer and that the E stood for Estelle. (For women living alone in the city only a first-name initial on mailboxes, in phone books—are there any left?—and the like is standard practice.) I hadn't yet logged the other names or perused the mailboxes.

Replicating, I assumed, her unctuous affect at the time, Ms. Belfer oozed, "'I'm Estelle. And you're?' After my charming request he said, 'I'm Conor.' 'What a beautiful name,' I said. 'So English, or is it Irish?' He didn't answer. He was at a loss for words, probably because I was so quick to recognize the name Conor as Irish. That's how I won that round."

"And you didn't press for his middle name?" I asked, in part to amuse myself but also because knowing Conor Congdon's middle name might facilitate finding him that much faster.

"No, I didn't. I didn't want him to think I was that interested. Then, as I recall, we went our separate ways. I mean, he did. He tore down the street. I stayed on the stoop."

That was the perfect lead-in to what I said next. "And now we'll go our separate ways, Ms. Belfer. I'm going to my apartment, and you'll stay on the stoop, I imagine."

"I think I will," she said, as if it was the weather that was keeping her there, as if she were needed to forestall the severest torrential downpour or tree-uprooting tornado that might have been gathering. "So," she said as I turned to leave, "you're sticking to your guns about this murder thing." She paused for a moment, put a right index finger to her rouged cheek. "Did you hear that? I said, 'sticking to your guns.' Isn't that like a pun or something?"

"Yes, Ms. Belfer, I think it is." I considered mentioning that many people think of puns as the lowest form of humor. I didn't for a couple reasons: (1) eager to get back to the computer, I didn't want to hang around anymore; (2) people who make that tiresome crack about puns are generally sticks-in-the-mud; and (3) I deal in puns all the time—and glad to do it.

At the computer within minutes, I googled C. F. Congdon and came up empty. Or so I thought. Lingering on the page to make certain I hadn't found a name I wanted so doggedly to find, I caught sight of Condon just above Congdon alphabetically. Condon. I tossed it around in my head. Maybe Conor F. Congdon was Condon. Was I stretching? Maybe not. Maybe Condon had been passing himself off as Congdon for some reason and doing as little of that as he could, if Ms. Belfer was any indication.

Since I had nothing else to go on, I thought, What do I have to lose? A couple of minutes at most. I had to explore all avenues, no matter how implausible. I clicked on Condon. The name Conor F. Condon came up. I clicked again and was linked to a brief *Dayton Daily News* item from a couple decades back. It seemed to have been excerpted from a society column. It relayed the news that Conor Condon, the champion Roth High School quarterback, had turned down an NFL bid in favor of attending college as preparation for a career in the law—"it's assumed he will eventually join his father's firm, Condon, Condon, Warwick and James."

A thousand-watt bulb went on over my head that threw light on Dayton, Ohio. Fulton Cutler's hometown. That was where he had been one of the twenty-member Fifth Street Fraternity, presumably a group of prominent local figures. Might not C. F.—Conor—Congdon have some connection to this Conor Condon?

But wait. Hadn't Ms. Belfer described Conor Congdon as a furtive animal? She had. Then again, Ms. Belfer had her debatable reasons for seeing people as she saw them.

If this Conor Condon was Congdon and had been a champion quarterback, he might have been a furtive, that's to say, threatening man. Some would say—sportswriters, for sure—that furtive is a valuable trait in a quarterback right up there with agility as the primary attribution. Then again, he could only have seemed furtive to her.

Also, if that Conor Condon had been eighteen or so then, he would have to have been forty or thereabouts when he lived in the murdered man's building. Ms. Belfer hadn't given an age for him, nor had I asked. Was the man Ms. Belfer waylaid, when she could, forty? If yes, he might have had twenty years to polish his off-the-field evasive manner.

And most strikingly, hadn't Ms. Belfer conjectured that her C. F. Congdon looked as if he might have played sports when he was a kid?

I knew what I had to do next. I wanted to quiz Ms. Belfer about Mr. Congdon's age. I was convinced she would have formed some opinion, perhaps more filtered than not. I could evaluate her brownstone-stoop conjectures.

Above and beyond that, I had an urge to look through Fulton Cutler's scrapbook again. For the most part, I'd still only skimmed the included obits. I wanted to look more closely at the names of the accumulating deceased.

It was getting late in the day, but I was fired up. I'd see if Ms. Belfer remained on her perch. If so, I'd prevail

on her to let me into the vaunted sanctuary. If she were
to insist on staying in the room and nattering, I'd put up
with it.

I grabbed my pad and pen and was out in lightning
speed. Ms. Belfer was as reliable as Lady Liberty holding
her torch in the harbor. I told her what I wanted to do.

Looking left and right to make certain she wasn't
being observed, she nodded at me to follow her.

In no time flat we were in Fulton Cutler's study with
the door shut—but not locked—behind us. I went directly
to the scrapbook, which, near as I could tell, was where
I'd left it at the end of our last visit.

"What are you trying to find out?" Ms. Belfer wanted
to know. She was perfectly within her rights to ask.

But I wasn't willing to tell her, which I saw as perfectly within my own rights. "If I find what I'm after, I'll
let you know," I said.

"You think the solution to the so-called murder is in
the scrapbook?"

"I'm not at liberty to say," I said, which I realized
implied that someone else could be involved with my
search. Of course, no one was. But maybe introducing a
speck of mystery on top of the core mystery would give
her something to think about quietly, distractedly.

Whether it worked, I can't say, but she did grow silent
while watching me. I did have a plan. It was even more

vital that I contact survivors mentioned in the later obituaries. They would know about the Condons.

I turned to the last six obits. I reasoned that the most recent had to be the obit preceding the one Fulton Cutler had not had the time to Flex Seal into the book. The other three or four would be the best bets for survivors' names, survivors who might have something, might have anything, to say about Fulton Cutler and his relationship to their dead relative and to a Condon with son Conor.

The veteran Tenth Precinct cop had said he remembered the Fulton Cutler investigation was carried out sometime in the spring. It follows that I was looking in the scrapbook for obits from June or May, April the latest, and others maybe a few months or years earlier.

Presto-chango! There was a May 30 obit for Chester Ingersoll Franklin. The obit gave the usual credits, death from a massive heart attack, the Fifth Street Fraternity membership—and the most germane facts for me just then, "Survivors include a son, Claude Martin Franklin, daughter Carole Franklin Barlow, and four grandchildren." Result: two leads in son Claude and daughter Carole.

I looked at the preceding two obits and culled Peter Preston Portman, sons Richardson, Amherst and Winthrop Portman; and Harrison Alan Newton, son Edmund, daughters Liesl Newton Sutton and Edith Newton. Result:

eight leads in Franklin son Claude, daughter Carole Barlow; Portman sons Richardson, Amherst and Winthrop; Newton son Edmund, daughters Liesl and Edith.

I scrawled all these down in my handy-dandy pad. They struck me as enough for my investigation in that direction.

I also couldn't miss Ms. Belfer holding the study door open and tapping the flip-flopped, imperfectly nail-polished toes of her right foot.

As I closed the scrapbook, I gave her a broad smile, thanked her for her patience, for her indulging me in my search.

I said we were ready to go.

"It's about time," she said, looking at her left wrist where she wore no watch.

The still operating grandfather clock against Fulton Cutler's wall said it was 7:51. (Who kept it wound—the stagers, Harold Swirner, Ms. Belfer?)

High time to go.

We parted on the stoop, Ms. Belfer curt—evidently, I hadn't thanked her sufficiently—and I as gracious as I could rally.

It wasn't early, and I was exhausted from a fact-packed day. I lay prostrate on my living room sofa for maybe an hour, paying no attention to the news I'd clicked on, downed a frozen dinner and went to bed just after nine. I didn't fall asleep when my head hit the pillow.

Hardly.

My mind was a black-gray-and-white kaleidoscope, thought patterns shifting like nobody's business. Here I was, wide-eyed and looking at the ceiling where light and shadows searched around in response to street traffic, Dayton, Ohio, names badmintoning around in my head.

Finally, I did fall asleep, and dreamed about trying to get into my own apartment—not the one I lived in but an apartment somewhere else with more rooms. I couldn't find the right key on a key ring holding too many keys to count.

FRIDAY

I awoke with a start, Dayton phone calls on my mind. It was 9:42. I'd slept for twelve hours. Are detectives, much less budding detectives, allowed that liberty? Still, was it too early to start? Could be. I always consider ten o'clock safer to begin phoning anyone. I threw on some clothes, went to the kitchen for orange juice, came back, consulted my list.

At 10:02 I was ready, primed. Could be all those sons and daughters whose names I'd written down might be difficult to track, but surely some would come through.

I won't itemize the sleuth-y rummaging I did, just report on individuals I did reach.

Which was enough.

When I got to the first one, Carole Franklin Barlow, I said I was an author writing a book about various obscure United States fraternities. It had come to my attention that Dayton had a fraternity about which I could turn up very little information—other than to have found her father's name in a *Dayton Daily News* obituary as a member of something called The Fifth Street Fraternity.

She bought the subterfuge and, in the tinkling voice of a woman in her forties or fifties, said—I was writing as fast as I could—"Oh, yes, my father was in that fraternity. He never talked about it much. So I don't know what I can tell you. Far as I remember, he formed it with a group of friends, and they set great store by it. The big thing about it was it was a secret society. They weren't supposed to talk about it. Not even with mother. Maybe he told her something, but we kids never heard about it, except how secret it was and that there was this big, big, extra secret they would never tell. All I remember is on a Wednesday night, off father would go and we'd all have to pretend we didn't notice. We did know the fraternity's name—The Fifth Street Fraternity—but we didn't know where on Fifth Street it was. For all I know, it wasn't even on Fifth Street. That might have been their little joke. That's the way father and his bigwig pals thought."

She stopped. I pressed on, "Did you happen to know the names of any of the other members?" I asked that in a non-fiction writer's matter-of-fact tone.

"I probably did at the time. It's so long ago now. I'm trying to think. I think Mr. Dougherty was one of them. Mr. Amerongen. Mr. Sotheby. We knew all father's friends, or most of them, but we weren't supposed to know they were all members. But we did and giggled about it. Among the wives—my mother, certainly—the whole thing was a giggle. You know, men things. It made them feel important, and, God knows, they needed to feel important."

"Do you remember if one of them was a Mister Con-don?"

"Oh, yes, Conrad Condon was one of them. He was a nice man. He'd stop by the house once in a while, some-times on a Wednesday. He and father would leave for the meeting, saying something or other about where they were going. To look something over. To put together a business plan. We'd look at each other and say, 'Gee, that sounds interesting' and giggle."

"Do you by any chance recall if Conrad Condon has a son? A son called Conor?"

"I sure do. Conor Condon, the big-wheel quarter-back. Father and Mr. Condon thought it would be nice for Conor and me to go out with each other. We did. About three times. Until I had enough."

Until she had enough. That rang a resounding bell with me: the supposed suicide note. Was having enough going to become a theme here? Of enough money? Could be.

Carole Franklin Barlow continued, "All Conor did was talk about himself and playing pro football. But he didn't. Play pro football. Mr. Condon put his foot down on any football after high school and college."

"Do you have any idea what happened to Conor Con-don?"

"Not a one, but surely you don't need this kind of information for your book."

"I did get off the track, didn't I, Ms. Barlow?" I said and tried to laugh it off. "I'm learning so many things about fraternities, I keep wanting to hear more."

"Like I said, Mr. Freund—did you say that's what your name is?—I'm afraid I can't tell you much more."

I told her she'd been immeasurably helpful, thanked her and hung up.

Next on the docket: Richard Portman. I got voicemail and left the message about my writing a book on obscure fraternities.

Edmund Newton, Harrison Newton's son, picked up the phone on the first ring and said a hurried "Hello." I had the impression he was eagerly, if not anxiously, expecting someone else.

I explained my made-up purpose and asked what he knew about his father's Fifth Street Fraternity. "That," he said harshly. He clearly didn't want anyone holding up his line. "We all took it as a joke. Behind Dad's back. Nothing much I can tell you, other than that. They called it a secret society. So it was all very secret. Some of them did try to get their sons to start their own, but the boys I knew then, and run into some of them today—who didn't flee Dayton when the fleeing was good—would humor them. We weren't interested. Con Condon, whose father was also Con, full name, Conrad Condon, was the only one of us who gave it a second thought. Con's full Christian first name was Conor."

I jumped on that like a fox on a chicken. "Conor Condon. I want to contact him, too."

"Good luck with that. Conor. Con, the Conster. You know how some names describe the person to a T? Con's nickname couldn't be more apt. He could con an Eskimo into giving him his igloo. He sure conned a lot of us. He even did a number on his late, great father." A short pause. "Look, I'm getting another call. I don't have much more to tell you anyway. Good luck with your book. I'll want to read it when it comes out."

He hung up, but no sooner did he brush me off than the phone rang. It was Richard Portman returning my call. I gave him the same song-and-dance about the book and asked about The Fifth Street Fraternity.

After he stopped laughing, which I estimate was close to a minute, he said, "The Fifth Street Fraternity. That's a laugh. It used to be, but we're not all laughing now. I know I just laughed about it. I guess it's still funny, but not funny-ha-ha. More like funny-peculiar. Maybe the only one who still thinks it's funny-ha-ha is Con Condon. Conor Condon."

"Yes?" I said, halting a gaze around the room I'd been giving myself as a break from the frantic notetaking. "Conor Condon. He's another son of a Fifth Street

Fraternity member I mean to contact. Why would he still think it's funny-ha-ha?"

"That's an easy one," Richard Portman came back with. "Because he took the money and ran." Again, he started laughing.

Money!

"Money? What money?" Exclaiming that, I straight-away was thinking money motive motive money.

"What money?" Richard Portman said with heartier laughter. "The tontine money. How many people have you talked to before me? Have you talked to any? Didn't any of them mention the money? Nobody brought up the nutty tontine?"

"As a matter of fact, no. No one did."

The "nutty tontine"?

Still laughing like a saw being bowed, he said, "Hmmm, nobody mentioned the tontine. It was the talk of Dayton. None of us had ever even heard of it when it first came to light. You probably never heard of it, either."

I did know what a tontine was. Is still, if the members of The Fifth Street Fraternity are to be credited. I had such a firm grasp on the meaning of a tontine that I was already more obdurately fixing on money motive motive money.

I'm not all that hip to obscure enterprises, but I call myself a writer because I started out as a reader, illogically, assuming, as a teenager, that if I was so sold on reading, I'd eventually become a writer.

Among the book genres with which I felt I ought to become acquainted were historical romances. I went through a spate of them, Kathleen Winsor's *Forever Amber* only the first. Does anyone but me remember that best-selling bodice-ripper, let alone Thomas B. Costain's *The Tontine* (tipping the scales at two volumes, approximately one thousand pages)?

"As a matter of fact," I said to Richard Portman, "I do know what a tontine is. A bunch of people put money in a pot that eventually, after the money is invested and appreciates, goes to the last of that group to remain alive."

"You got it," Richard Portman said. He'd stopped laughing. "I lied before. None of us knew what it was except for Mrs. Peabody, Charlie Peabody's wife, and my friend Army Peabody's mother. The way it goes is that Mrs. Peabody had read a novel about tontines. She told Mr. Peabody about it, and he told his secret-loving friends about it when they were putting together the damn-fool fraternity we all got such a kick out of. They said why not do the same thing?"

"And they did," I said.

"Damn right, they did. And swore each other to secrecy about it. You mean, nobody you've talked to told you about it at all? It was all anybody talked about for weeks after Con's dad died."

"It was a surprise to everybody? Nobody knew about it?"

"Nobody was supposed to know about it. A few people did. Some of the members were better than others at keeping secrets. Conrad Condon wasn't one of the tough-minded secret keepers. Conman Con conned the whole tontine thing out of his father. Like father, like son. Maybe Con wasn't the only one. A few secrets got out. It wasn't much of a secret that they all drank and smoked cigars. Phallic, if you ask me. Con liked the idea, not of smoking cigars. He liked drinking, an AA candidate in the making, which his father reamed him out for. The hypocrite. He was a worse lush. A do-as-I-say-not-as-I-do guy. But tontines. Conor liked that idea a lot. His dad was urging him to form his own club. Everybody thought Conrad controlled Con's every move. He did, too. If he didn't, Con would have been playing in the NFL and not flunking out of law school. We all think dad told son about the tontine to get him stoked on following through with a chip-off-the-old-block fraternity. It never happened. Conman became too much infatuated with the road."

About now I was thinking I had struck metaphoric oil. There was so much to unpack in Richard Portman's aria-with-laugh-track that I was momentarily unsure about where to begin. There was one phrase that stuck like a burr to wool trousers: "flunking out of law school." You mean that after brushing off the football offer, this Con Conor kid listened to his father—under how much pressure?—and then didn't cut it?

"Conor Condon had to leave law school?" I said to Richard Portman when he stopped to take a breath. "Do you happen to know what he did then, where he is now? I've been trying to find him. Uh, for the book. You said he took the tontine money and ran. Do you have any idea where?"

"Sorry. I can't help you there. God knows where he is. I don't think anyone in Dayton knows. At least, nobody here has said anything to me about hearing from Con, the people still here who know—well, knew—him. I can tell you that after he flunked out of law school, he was back for a while, but it was pretty obvious his father wasn't all that delighted to have him around. People would see the two of them in restaurants and like that, either arguing or not talking at all. I saw them once at Marion's—a great place for pizza if you don't know it—and I had to pretend not to see them. You never saw Mrs. Condon with them. You wouldn't. I wonder if she even knew about what went on at those fraternity—ha!—meetings. You'd hear all sorts of things. They got naked. They had hookers. They played gin rummy. They skipped rope. That was one of the wildest. Anyway, after a while, Con left town. Word got around that Conrad gave him money to go away and stay away. He did, for forever.

"Check that. Not forever. Every once in a while, he'd show up in Dayton and hang around for a few weeks. I ran into him, it's got to be at least twelve or fifteen years ago at Marion's, of all places. I didn't see him, but he saw me and sat down uninvited—not that I would have sent him away. He joked about the old days. In high school I was on the football team with him. He was hot stuff. After we got that good-old-days talk out of the way, he got around to telling me where he'd been for the last few years. Taking a job here and there. Temporary. He said he was too eager to live the high life than hang around one place for too long. I'm trying to think of where he said he'd been. Chicago, if I remember right, Detroit, New Orleans."

I saw fit to interrupt. "Did he ever mention living in New York City, Manhattan?"

"Not that I recall. No, he never mentioned New York. I'm sure about that."

He might not have, would he? Richard Portman was talking about some time before Con Condon set up house under Ms. Belfer's keen eye.

I asked, "And Marion's was the last time you saw him?"

"I didn't ever seek him out, you understand. We had

our own—I don't know—issues I won't go into. Well, girls we dated. Marion's was the last time I saw him. Others saw him other times. I'd see people and they'd say, 'Con Condon's back in town. Did you see him?' and I'd say no, and they'd say, 'Still the same old Conman, maybe a little the worse for wear.'

"I can tell you the last time I heard about him being here. Around the time his father died. Maybe he heard his dad was not in good shape and came back to be with him. A lot of people saw him at the funeral. I didn't go. And I guess he stayed around for the will to be read and for the tontine money to come to him. The tontine money that he knew was coming to him. Nobody knew how much, but it had to be plenty, money up the wazoo. Then he left. Zip, he was gone."

"And you don't know if anyone has heard from him? How about his mother?"

"I was never really in touch with Con's mother. If anyone here has heard from Con and knows where he is, I haven't heard about it. Tell you the truth, I haven't given the Conman any thought until you called me out of the blue. If you need him for your book, you're going to have to find him some other way."

I couldn't think of anything else to ask Richard Portman, thanked him for his time and for the great help he'd been and hung up. If he'd mentioned nothing more than the tontine business, I'd have been grateful. I suppose I could have called some of the others I'd written down and had the tontine aspect confirmed.

No need to do that. The three Daytonians I quizzed told me more than enough to go on.

I did think it might be illuminating to access the *Dayton Daily News* archives. It wouldn't be a bad idea, I said to myself, to search out a Fifth Avenue Fraternity obit that might have run not too long before Fulton Cutler had his final farewell.

I googled, and only eight weeks before, about the time Conor Congdon likely moved to Ms. Belfer's bailiwick, Fifth Avenue Fraternity member John Milton Mosley was lowered into Dayton ground.

C. F. Congdon, né Conor Condon, may have left Dayton, Ohio, to travel single-o, but he certainly managed to keep his lucrative birthplace in mind.

Thinking about that, I decided why not contact someone at *Dayton Daily News* directly to see if they'd covered the Fifth Avenue Fraternity's tontine revival.

I was put through to someone on the city desk. "City desk, Hafetz speaking, how can I help?"

I told No-First-Name Hafetz—standard newsroom talk, of course—about the book I was (not) writing on obscure fraternities and their quirky practices, if any. I said I'd learned that the now defunct Fifth Street

Fraternity became defunct with the death of Conrad Condon, the last member. One Conrad Condon fact I hadn't
learned was a middle name. I wouldn't have, since no one
I'd spoken to had mentioned it, nor had I seen an obituary. I wouldn't have known to look for it. That was a lie,
but I held on to it.

When it comes to lying, I was becoming a past master.

"Mr. Hafetz," I dug in, "I'm informed that Conrad
Condon was the last member of The Fifth Street Fraternity to die and had therefore received the tontine money."

Hafetz cut in. "The tontine money. Right. The carload
of cash that had been building up from the members'
initial money deposit. You know it was a secret society,
right?"

I muttered "Right."

"The fraternity was established before my time. I'm
not originally from Dayton, but I knew about it. Who
didn't? The older they got, the members strutted around
town as if they were bigger muckety-mucks than they
really were.

"If you want to know, they were little short of a laughingstock. Which isn't to say they weren't prominent in
their way. Some of their obituaries even ran on our front
page, Conrad Condon, for one. Always below the fold.

"And then there was this tontine thing, which was
supposed to be their secret society's biggest secret. It

wasn't. I'm told there were rumors about it for years. The paper was never able to confirm it. So we kept it out of their obits. We had to. Some of them were advertisers. None of them ever worked at the paper.

"We only published something about the tontine when it was out in the open. I can tell you it was all the way out in the open, thanks to Conrad Condon's son, who came into the money when his father died and the will was read. Some freakin' gamble.

"So there was all this talk about tontines, and because there was such curiosity, we did run a piece on the history of tontines, the kind of assignment you hand an intern. We pegged it to The Fifth Street Fraternity, of course. Too bad we couldn't include how much that tontine was worth, but if anyone knew other than the Condon boy, nobody was saying. You can find the piece in the archives."

I included that in the notes. I was talking so fast my wrist was incipient carpal-tunneling.

"One thing we didn't do," newsman Hafetz chugged on, "was mention the son's name in the article. It was in there, but we edited it out. He'd gotten enough attention for himself without us adding to it. Look, Mr. Freund, I'd like to talk to you for the rest of the day, but my phone is ringing off the hook here. The last thing I'll tell you is when Condon's son left town soon after the father died, you heard a lot of good riddances. He was a big football hero in his day, but, like they say, fame is fleeting. We see that at the paper all the time. Okay, Mister Freund? Goodbye and good luck."

Click.

He was gone. I suppose I'd found out enough from him about Dayton's reaction to the tontine. About Conor Condon I'd also learned something: how he was regarded. I'd learned nothing of his whereabouts, which are what I believed was most important to discover.

My mind was also running back on the phone calls I'd spent the past couple of hours making. I had no idea what the callees looked like, but as we all do, I had images in my head. Were I ever to write this all up, I might want to find some way to describe them. This wasn't my plan, but then, it's never a mistake to plan for the unknown.

For *Dayton Daily News* city-desk vet Hafetz, I'd initially pictured him with green-billed visor and armband but dismissed it. I was thinking of the dark ages. City rooms haven't looked like that for decades. This modern-day Hafetz I saw was in his mid-to-late forties, narrow head, faced lined before his time. I granted him the cigarette hanging from his mouth as in the olden days but unlit, in keeping with today's no-smoking workplace rules.

I was pulling Richard Portman's image from whatever part of the brain where images develop—the cerebellum?—when the reverie was quashed by the phone.

I picked up the receiver and heard—harshly, I might add—"Daniel Freund. Izzy Abramovitz." This was the Izzy Abramovitz who'd told me not to get back in touch with him under, he'd threateningly implied, pain of death. It couldn't be any other Izzy Abramovitz, not with that don't-speak-to-me-till-I-tell-you-to-speak tone.

He pushed on. "What I have to say isn't gonna be easy for me, so don't interrupt." As if I were even thinking of it. Part of me was still grappling with hearing from him at all. "The Flex Seal tub, the Elmer's Glue-All. You got me to thinkin' about 'em. Why hadn't I thought about 'em until you brought 'em up."

He said this all but accusatorily, as if I had no right to bring them up. I kept my mouth shut clamshell tight. "And things started coming back to me. Fingerprints. I remembered we'd had the Flex Seal tub brushed for fingerprints. None.

"Because it was such an obvious open-and-shut case and nothing on the desk or the Flex Seal on the floor indicated otherwise, we didn't see any reason to look in the desk drawers. If we had, we'd've seen the Elmer's Glue-All and found the dead man Cutler's fingerprints on it. If we checked it now, we'd find your fingerprints and his on it. So what was the Flex Seal doing there?

"What's it doing on the desk now? How much glue do you need to paste an obituary into a scrapbook? That's what I want to know. What was I thinking? Maybe I wasn't thinking. That's why I'm calling you now. You're not saying anything. Cat got your tongue?"

He stopped, abruptly. For much of these late morning frothings, he'd let up on his standard attack mode, but with the last couple of remarks he resumed the signature commandant's stance. I felt like someone backed into a corner suddenly allowed, expected, to explain himself.

"If you're not going to say anythin'," Izzy Abramovitz resumed, "I'm gonna tell you why I'm callin' after I said I wouldn't. And meant it, I don't need to add. But, like I said, you got me thinkin', and I gotta say I wasn't wrong about the Cutler case at the time, but I might be wrong about it now."

I wasn't about to take a poke at that logic, if logic was at all applicable.

"Here's what I wanna do," he graveled.

He dictated. I listened.

"I want to see that room again, and I want you to come with me. Ms. Belfer can let us in with her keys. I know she has 'em. You may think you fooled me the last time. You didn't. I know you been diggin' around, but you probably ain't figured anythin' else out."

I'd "figured" a good deal out, but until I saw him, I wasn't going to bring him up to speed. I had to keep some weighty things to myself.

He raced on. "I want to get this done. It's eatin' at me. I'm lookin' at the clock now. It's close to noon. It'll take me an hour or so to get there. Let's say I meet you at the building at, okay, 1:30. We can count on Ms. Belfer bein' there. If she's not, we'll buzz her. It won't take long."

Without so much as another flaming word he rang off.

I was in front of the building at 1:25, where, predictably Ms. Belfer—like an old-time French concierge—was stationed. Izzy Abramovitz was also there, not exactly tapping his toe but looking as if he could be the toe-tapping type when pressed. It's a trait Ms. Belfer and he could have in common.

Without further ado, as Izzy Abramovitz was anything but the ado type, and neither was Ms. Belfer, we returned to Fulton Cutler's study. "All right, let's get to this Flex Seal business," he said.

That's after he dismissed Ms. Belfer, insisting that she stand guard outside the apartment door to stop anyone else entering. As if anyone else would likely try. Given a chore, Ms. Belfer put up less of a fuss than I expected.

He stomped to the desk, on those shod feet of his that I was beginning to regard as not so much heavy as anvil-esque. He didn't pick up the heavy-duty container but leaned toward it with his laser stare. Was he thinking it might tell him something?

Foolish of me to believe it might not. For as I joined

in staring, something struck me—again, I might add—that struck Izzy Abramovitz just about simultaneously. When Izzy Abramovitz got the tacit Flex Seal message, he blurted, "I want to know why anyone would use this glop in a scrapbook."

I realized that though I'd had the thought before, I hadn't articulated it to myself. I don't normally smite my forehead, and I didn't then. Neither did Izzy Abramovitz. But before he said any more, I said, "You wouldn't use this glop."

He said, "You'd use it for somethin' different, which is why it wasn't on the desk when us precinct know-it-alls came in the room. It was never on the desk. Whoever the *shmendrik* was who put it on the desk for show when we returned it to the room got it wrong."

When Izzy Abramovitz said that, I swear I heard a fillip in my head. I trotted to the window with the unlocked latch. I knew about Conor "The Conman" Condon, didn't I? "Why isn't this window able to be opened?" I asked.

Izzy Abramovitz hotfooted it to the window and said, "You got something there, boychik. I was just thinking the same thing."

Whether he was or he wasn't, I'll never know. Instead, I said, "Are you also thinking what I'm thinking—?"

"—that if the heavy Flex-thing goo," Izzy Abramovitz yelped, "was used on the window, that's why and how the murderer got into the room and got out?" He was not near the window, nor did he come over to try it, let alone apply any of his conspicuous force to open it.

"That's what I'm thinking," I said. If ever I was in the position to one-up Izzy Abramovitz, this was it. "The murderer used this window. And I have a pretty good idea who the murderer had to be."

"You do, huh?" Izzy Abramovitz came back with, as if he was in no mood to be one-upped now. Or ever. "Who was it, wise guy?"

"Conor Condon," I said, resolutely crossing Amy Pritchard and George Reiser off my to-do list. Money motive motive money took precedence, had to. Plain as day that Izzy Abramovitz, Chief Honcho of the Money Motive Squad, would have none of them.

"Yeah, and just who is this Conor—is that his name?— this Conor Condon character, and how did you smoke him out?"

"I haven't smoked him out," I said, attempting to be momentarily lowkey. "Not yet. I don't have any idea how to smoke him out."

"Let's not worry about that right now, buddy boy," Izzy Abramovitz said. "If we need to smoke anybody out, I can take care of that. Just tell me who this guy is and be quick about it. I don't have all day."

"Okay," I said, an urge to rub it in rising. "If you'd

have looked at the scrapbook, as I did, you would have noticed that the only things in it were obituaries."

"So, Cutler was dead as a doornail. What's that got to do with the price of baloney?"

"Lots," I said, with the rubbing-in urge lifting ever higher. "They're all from the *Dayton Daily News*, which is where Fulton Cutler was born, and they are all obituaries for members of something called The Fifth Street Fraternity. Fulton Cutler was one of the twenty members."

"He was keeping track of old friends. What about it? People do that when they get old. I used to run into it all the time—suspects, witnesses. That's a laugh. Old friends." He sneered. "What are they good for? Usually lookin' for handouts."

Izzy Abramovitz was going to make this hard for me. I knew how to handle it. I was going to save the best for last. "Yes, well," I said, "all these old friends had established a tontine, and—."

"A what?"

"A tontine," I said, as if it were a matter of renowned fact. "Oh, you might not know what a tontine is."

"Don't get smart-alecky with me, boy. I don't know what the fuck a tontine is. Tell me, and tell me fast, before I lose my temper. That's not somethin' you want to see."

I'd done enough rubbing-in, so hurriedly explained "tontine" to him, finishing with, "Looking at the obituaries revealed to me that only minutes before he was shot, Fulton Cutler must have been about to paste up an obit for the eighteenth deceased member. So Conrad Condon and Fulton Cutler were the last surviving members. That's why Fulton Cutler was killed."

Izzy Abramovitz was giving this thought. "That's a theory. I grant you that much, kid."

As I said, I was saving the best for last. That's when I announced, "And, it's the undeniably correct theory. What would you say, Izzy, if I told you that at the time Fulton Cutler's life was clipped like all the obits in his scrapbook, the man living in the apartment directly below this one was someone passing himself off as C. F. Congdon?"

"Did you just say Congdon with a G?" Izzy Abramovitz wanted to know. "It could just be coincidence." He wasn't going to give me anything.

"I thought that, too," I said. "I checked. He's the same Conor Condon. I don't think you'll be surprised to hear he turns out to be the only son of Conrad Condon. No Conrad Condon daughters, either. The *Dayton Daily News* had information on him. Even more of his contemporaries and his father's contemporaries had much to say about Conor. He was known to everyone I spoke to in Dayton as a bad boy who collected the tontine prize money after his father died. Of supposedly poor health."

"You found out about all this and didn't let me know?"

"You said if I came up with anything else to leave you out of it."

When Izzy Abramovitz became flushed, which was now, he turned rose-red, the wrinkles adding to the petal similarity. "How much do I have to explain to you, boychik? What I meant was, if you come up with anythin' else of no consequence, don't let me know. What you just told me is important. It's the kind of evidence you need to understand is important. I see it even if you don't."

What do you say to that? What I said was, "I suppose I should have."

"What else can you tell me? Don't tell me you located the guy, and you're keeping that from me, too. Naw, you already said you don't know where he is. But before we get to that, we gotta assume if Fulton Cutler was murdered—okay, he was—that's gonna make this Con guy the prime suspect, our prime suspect. Mine and yours. He had the motive for murder. The money. Nine times out of ten it's money. Make that nine and a half times. You got that?"

"I got it," I said, and thought that even if I might have mentioned Amy Pritchard and George Reiser to corroborate my thoroughness on potential motives, I wasn't about to now.

"Good. Don't forget it. What about that money? How much did the tontine thing add up to?"

"Nobody seems to know," I said and regretted I hadn't

been able to nail down a sum. "They assumed it was plenty. Who knows how much?"

"Did they assume it?" Izzy Abramovitz wanted to know, "or did you?"

"Both," I admitted. "Would anybody want to commit a murder for less?"

"That goes to show what a rookie you are," Izzy Abramovitz said with glee flooding his round, rose-petal face. "I've worked cases where people killed for much less. I once worked a case where some *shlemiel* was offed over a Fudgsicle."

He emitted one of his raucous guffaws. "So we get down to business." He didn't rub his hands together. He might as well have. "Now we have our prime suspect. You could say we know who done it. What we gotta do now is work out how he done it and until this minute got away with it. Any ideas, boy-o?"

While Izzy Abramovitz was spraying the air with spittle—I know, I know; I've left that part out about him until now—I'd been doing some thinking on my own. It looked as if I had just progressed from the mystery writer's whodunit phase to the mystery writer's howdhedunit phase.

I had my idea and was prepared to set it before Izzy Abramovitz like a warm apple pie. I affected an air of confiding to him. "It's the Flex Seal that gave me the first potent clue, although it didn't occur to me why until just this minute. I should have seen it when I first saw the Elmer's glue in the drawer, where the scissors were probably also kept. If Fulton Cutler used the Elmer's to paste in the obits, then the Flex Seal had to be used for something else. Like what? What would need that kind of strength? What about that window?"

I pointed at the window with the missing latch. "I figured maybe the window wouldn't stay shut. Maybe Fulton Cutler, who didn't like repairmen coming in and out—Ms. Belfer told me that—decided he'd fix it himself and got the Flex Seal.

"But if that were so, his fingerprints would have been on the container. They weren't. Someone else who took care not to leave fingerprints had to be in the room, someone who brought the Flex Seal with him and forgot to take it when he left and had sealed the window shut. How did he get in in the first place? We know it wasn't through the study door.

"I say he locked the door to give the locked-room impression. I had already looked at what was in the garden. I saw the tree with the cut-off branches. Had he climbed the tree and then had the branches sawed off later? Maybe.

"Then I saw the ladder leaning against the back garden wall. I figure he had noticed when he was in the yard that Fulton Cutler often left the window open. Con Conor had to have noticed that Fulton Cutler stayed up late, doing whatever he did. The chance of anybody seeing him on the ladder or pulling himself into the room was small. Even if someone did, he or she wouldn't likely do anything about it. New Yorkers are like that.

"He came in through the open window, shot Fulton Cutler, pressed the gun handle round the dead man's right hand and let it drop. Then he went to swab the windowsill, climbed out, forgot the Flex Seal until it was too late, put the ladder back against the garden wall, went inside, took off his gloves, and that was that."

I took some pride in my nonstop explication and waited for Izzy Abramovitz's acknowledgment. I didn't have to wait long. He regarded me with an expression somewhere between glower and surprise.

He said, with a look of vindictive joy, "That's exactly what I came up with. I've coached you better than I thought. You did leave two things out. What are they?"

I wondered what they were, but only after I thought that three springs earlier Izzy Abramovitz hadn't given over too much time to looking out the window at the garden. He'd been wedded to his open-and-shut case, which precluded much, if any, garden gazing. Since I'd been in the room, I hadn't noticed his giving the garden more than a cursory glance.

"You're not volunteering those two things you

missed," Izzy Abramovitz said with bated breath. "I guess I'm going to have to spell them out. One, you didn't point out that there's no such thing as the perfect murder. Murderers always make a mistake. That's one hundred percent true. Trust me on this, like everything else I tell you. Someday I'll write a book all about it. Or maybe you'll write it for me. The Flex Seal was Condon's. You mentioned it but not as the incriminating mistake. You know what the other is? You don't. I can tell. The suicide note. The 'I've had enough of this.'"

Yes, the suicide note, written on Fulton Cutler stationery in his handwriting, which had been verified. I'd never factored that in.

"Gotcha there, don't I?" Izzy Abramovitz said, black eyes beaming. "Howdya account for that?"

Not for the first time with him, I was at a loss for words. I didn't scratch my head but was tempted to. "I don't know," I replied and hurriedly added, "Do you?"

"No, boychik, I don't know, but I have a hunch, and my hunches pay off one hundred percent. Whaddaya think it is?"

Just then I came up short on my supply of hunches but felt impelled to say something. Lacking one, I tried, "Something to do with fingerprints?"

"Not bad," Izzy Abramovitz said, "for a newbie. Yup, fingerprints got something to do with it. Cutler's fingerprints were on it. And someone else's. We didn't make too much of it at the time. We figured Cutler might not have been the only one to handle his stationery. The cleaning lady could've moved the stack. We were gonna fingerprint her, but then we didn't bother. So where does that leave us? Come on, boy, come on. This is a murder we're talking about."

He put me on the spot. No, more like he kept me on the spot. More leftfield tries required. I jumped in with, "The murderer saw the stationery, took a sheet and dictated 'I've had enough of this.'"

"You think a murderer, this Con Condon, was gonna take that kind of time?" Hadn't I already ruled that out myself? Why was I dredging it up now? "Another thing. If a man is writing with a .38 to his head, that's going to show up in his handwriting. Try again, boy-o."

Then it hit me. "I know this is going to sound far-fetched, but Con Condon had the note with him. He found it somewhere, found it on someone's table or bureau or desk or somewhere, put on gloves to handle it but couldn't get rid of the second set of fingerprints without rubbing out Fulton Cutler's fingerprints. So what? He brought the note with him."

"Now you're ridin' a buckin' bronco," Izzy Abramovitz said. "He brought it with him."

"You mean, the note might have been the whole idea behind the murder?"

"Whaddaya think, Daniel Freund?"

"I think, why does Fulton Cutler send a suicide note to someone else. So it has to be Conman Condon's father."

"Conman?"

"Dayton people call him that."

"You're telling me he already has a record."

"An unofficial one."

"You're on to somethin' there, boy-o. Why does a man send a suicide note to someone else? I'm gonna say in the history of suicide notes, this has to be a first. But it's startin' to hit me." With that, Izzy Abramovitz went literal and hit his right temple with the bottom of his right palm, an honest-to-god smite. "But hold on. We're gettin' ahead of ourselves here."

I registered his use of "we."

"What we gotta do," Izzy Abramovitz issued, "is track this Conman Condon down." He sent me another of his glowers. "Or did you already, and are just holding out on me?"

"No, Izzy, all I know is what the Daytonians —a couple of them—told me."

"Did I tell you you could call me Izzy? Right, I did, Go ahead."

"Shortly after his father died, Con Condon took his inheritance, the tontine money and skipped town. Nobody knows where. I had the impression nobody wants to know. Or cares."

"We care, boy-o. We got our murderer, but all we got here is circumstantial evidence. It's not an open-and-shut case—a reopened-and-shut case—until we have the Condon lug in hand and confessin'. There is one little thin' in our favor. Do ya know what that is?"

I didn't and nodded to that effect.

"He thinks he's gotten away with it, which means he'll get cocky about it. He already has, you can bet on it. He'll get sloppy about it. He already has, another winnin' bet. That's what they do, ya know. Especially this kinda fool if what you tell me is true. They get careless. They're careless people."

"Careless people"—straight from F. Scott Fitzgerald. I envisioned a paperback book smiling on an end table a few houses away.

"They let things slip. Sometimes they go so far they even boast about it. We got that on him."

Izzy Abramovitz was on a roll. I was ready to roll with him, although I wasn't ready, as he was, to charge around the study like a bull looking for a china shop. As he pursued his hyperactive rant and rave, standing in place was good enough for me.

"Okay, awright, okay, what do we do next?" he raved. "We find the sonuvabitch. And how do we do that?"

"He could be anywhere," I threw in. "When he was drifting around, from time to time he told people back in Dayton places where he went, and he was all over the place. This is before he got the tontine money. From what I can tell, nobody back there has heard from him at all."

"Fuck it," Izzy Abramovitz said and furrowed his furrowed brow further. "We do got a few things on our side, sonny boy. You say he used the last name Congdon when he lived downstairs. "It worked for him here. The obvious thing—maybe too obvious—is that he's lazy enough to use it again. Some jerks get their highs thinking up new names. Others think they have better things to do with their time. Let's hope he's one of the lazy ones." He thought for a second. "Let's get outta here. I got somethin' I gotta do."

He was already leaving the study and the apartment. I followed him, allowing a last look to see if I needed to tidy anything. I didn't.

Izzy Abramovitz stopped at the former Fulton Cutler apartment front door long enough to compliment Mr. Belfer on being a "first-rate watch dog." Ms. Belfer swapped nothing in return. She was trying to decide if she'd just been called a dog. She had been.

When we got to the street—Ms. Belfer, still flummoxed, hovering at the top of the stoop—Izzy Abramovitz said to me, "I'm going to get some information. Where can I reach you when I have it?"

"I'll be home, right there." I pointed at my building. "You have the phone number."

"I just called you on it," Izzy Abramovitz said, not without some satisfaction.

"Is that a cell phone? You don't have a cell phone?"

"I do." I pulled out my pad and pen and wrote down both numbers this time.

"I know what you mean," Izzy Abramovitz said. "I hate my cell phone, too. I have more in common than I woulda thought with someone like you." I ignored that—or tried to. "I'm goin' down the street to the precinct now. I got somethin' I need to do there. If Doyle is there—he should be—he'll help."

"Desk sergeant Doyle," I said, like an idiot. "I know him. He's the one who told me to contact you. Maybe I can come with you."

I was thinking that showing up there with Izzy Abramovitz would confirm my seriousness.

"All the more reason you don't come," Izzy Abramovitz said, looking as if he'd just escaped a narrow one. "You go home like a good boy. I'll call when I have somethin'." He thought for a minute. "Where is home?"

I poked a thumb in the direction of my building—again—and added, "That one there."

"I'll ring your bell, and you can let me up."

He'd said enough, ankled on the anvil feet and

hustled to, and across, Eighth Avenue. I watched him head toward the precinct. I was tempted to follow him but thought better of it. That's not what good boys do.

Good boys go home. I went home. I looked at the clock: 2:57. I couldn't think of anything other than what had just happened and what might happen next. I saw the 1953 *Great Gatsby* edition lying where I'd first left it four days earlier. I had the fleeting thought that perhaps the edition could fill me in on what next. It didn't. Outside of a soothing, low-decibel purr, it wasn't able to lend that hypothesis any credence.

I sat in my reading chair, not reading but thinking. What was Izzy Abramovitz up to? I thought I knew. Surely, if desk sergeant Doyle was at the precinct—even if he weren't—Izzy Abramovitz could gain access to the Fulton Cutler open-and-shut case record. Why he would want to review it, I couldn't guess. He no longer credited it. Or might he be looking it over to confirm that he had been right the first time and therefore could brush off boychik-boy-o as a pushy upstart, a fiction writer in over his head, a jerk with nothing else to do.

But what about the Flex Seal? He had conceded that in his hurry to label the case open-and-shut, he'd ignored that very visible (too visible?) clue. On the other hand, the suicide note—should I put that in quotes?—was there, had been there all the time, hadn't been brought along by any *fakakta* murderer. Or had it?

I was running these thoughts back and forth in my head when the door buzzer jolted me out of them. I looked at my watch—4:33. It had to be Izzy Abramovitz. I buzzed him in. He arrived, puffing, at my open door.

"You mighta told me you live on the second floor. Those stairs are killers." I was on the verge of apologizing, but he wanted none of that. He hurried into the apartment, gave it a onceover. "What's with all the books? Right, you're a writer, but who knows when you get the time to write when you're doin' so much readin'? Don't tell me. I have things to tell you. Do you have anything to drink? Water? Anything. Schnapps? Water's fine."

He sat down in the reading chair, gave his surroundings the hard look detectives might give as a matter of policy when entering a new environment. He even took in the now docile *Great Gatsby* 1953. "I see you're readin' *The Great Gatsby*. I saw the movie, didn't think much of it."

I looked at the book for a reaction—none—and went to get Izzy Abramovitz his glass of water.

He talked. "You won't believe this. Maybe you will. You'll want to. I located Conor Condon. You'd be surprised what you can do in a precinct. Maybe you wouldn't."

I brought him the water. He downed it in one mighty sip.

"My instincts didn't fail me," he went on. "Okay, some of them were yours. You'll never guess where he is."

He handed me the glass, indicated he wanted more. He kept talking, while I refilled the glass. "He's in Manhattan. See, that's what I'm talkin' about. These guys who think they got away with murder think they can get away with murder. If you know what I'm sayin'. Cocksure, the lot of 'em. He got caught in some sorta drivin' charge. A fender-bender or the like. Gave 'im enough of a police record so he could be turned up. He was using the name—get this—Congdon, but his Ohio driver's license was Condon. Nothin' illegal enough about it to get him in more hot water. He only had to pay the ticket. Did you ever find out what the 'F' stood for? Might be innerestin' to know, might not be."

"I never did," I said and silently agreed with myself that it might be innerestin' to know, might not be at this point.

"Leastways, this was a year ago. I say he's livin' in Manhattan, but he could've moved. He gave his address as 312 West Eighty-eighth Street. He also gave a phone number. I wrote it down. No, I didn't. Doyle did and gave it to me."

Izzy Abramovitz fumbled in his pockets, produced

nothing. "Don't worry. It's here." He stopped fumbling. "Here's the thing. We hope he's still on West Eighty-eighth Street. We track him there. We only have the circumstantial evidence. So, boy-o, we have to get him to spill his guts. Which he isn't inclined to do, is he?"

He was looking to me to say no. I said, "Did you tell Sergeant Doyle why you were looking up Conor Condon?"

"Why would I? The name would mean nothin' to 'im. And if I did, he'd think I was in cahoots with you. I didn't want 'im thinking I was loony, too. We're on our own here. Just like we want to be. At least for the time being. We'll bring active cops in when we're good and ready. The thing we gotta come up with right now, boy-o, is a scheme. Any ideas?"

Izzy Abramovitz was asking me for ideas. Did I have any? I came up with, "Case the joint?"

"That's a start. Tell you what. It's after five. We don't want to go for it now." He handed me the empty glass in the manner of a member facing an attendant at a gentlemen's club. "I'm gonna leave. I'll pick you up bright and early tomorrow morning, eight a. m. I drive a gray Honda Civic, if you know what that is." I didn't. When I was a kid, every fall I knew all the new models. No more. I had other fish to fry. "A 2008 model. Doesn't matter. Be in front of your building. I'll honk."

He was already at the door and, without saying any

more, out of it. The noise he made plodding down the stairs could have frightened the neighbors but didn't seem to. He hadn't mentioned a car before. I'd assumed he'd come on the subway for the Fulton Cutler exploration, but maybe he'd driven the 2008 Honda Civic. Maybe he still had some sort of police decal and was able to use one of the angled packing spaces in front of the precinct. There's a handy perk for you.

I didn't spend too much time thinking about that. I microwaved another frozen dinner, made a few calls to friends I'd been neglecting—giving no information about what I'd been up to—and went to bed. I read. No, I didn't read, but I tried to. What would I read that would take my mind off the impending 312 West Eighty-eighth joint case? Not *The Great Gatsby*. When I went to my bookcases, I heard odd clucking sounds from the end table and gave up.

I set my alarm for 7:30, and after imagining any number of calamitous scenarios, fell asleep. If I dreamed—of Con Conor, Izzy Abramovitz or both—I have no recollection.

SATURDAY

Like a good boy, I was at the top of my stoop next morning ten minutes before eight. I waved to Ms. Belfer at the top of hers. A gray car I took to be the Honda Civic 2008 model cruised down the street: Izzy Abramovitz early to catch me out, I assumed. I was not to be intimidated and descended the stoop stairs hastily to be ready for hopping in, which I did.

I didn't look to see whether Ms. Belfer was keeping track. I had no doubt she was, but she may not have been able to verify Izzy Abramovitz as the motorist. As a card-carrying petty person, I'm more than petty enough to have taken satisfaction in that.

Izzy Abramovitz got right to the morning's agenda, as he was not a man for small talk. For him, chitchat was a waste of his unreclaimable time. I agree with him. Even the word "chitchat" gets on my nerves.

I'd barely secured the seatbelt when Izzy Abramovitz announced, "Here's how I see it. We park on West Eighty-eighth Street with a good view of 312. Don't tell me you know this is called surveillance. I'm not innerested in what you know about how cops work." I was about to say no such thing, but he'd formed his opinion. All I could do was go along with it. "What do the brainy guys call that kind of shop talk? Jargon?"

He was making good time against the uptown morning traffic. He'd plainly put the Honda Civic through its paces in the years he had it.

When I got in, he was removing some newspapers—the *Daily News*, some others—from the right-hand front seat. In the divider between the two seats, there was an open Coors beer in one of the cup holders. In the other one was a Binaca sprayer. There was a mezuzah—if you can believe it—hung on a string from the rearview mirror. I can only describe the prevalent odor as eau de Izzy Abramovitz. God only knows how he'd maintained and maneuvered a police car with a siren at the ready but maybe no cup holders.

Turning onto West Eighty-eighth Street, he jockeyed into the parking space he wanted on the north side of the street. On Saturday, alternate side of the street parking is suspended, and parking spaces are as hard to find as Indian pennies.

"That was lucky," I was dumb enough to say.

"Luck has nothing to do with it." He fixed me with the black beacons. "Here's what we do first off. You get out of the car and go check the mailboxes or directory or whatever they have at 312. You know what you're looking for. If a guy who looks like Conor Condon comes out while you're looking, don't do anything. If he asks what you're doing, tell him you're looking for...make up a name. You write fiction. You oughta be able to do that. Then tell him you must have the wrong address and walk away. But not to the car."

I had my marching orders. I undid the seatbelt, got out and walked with a certain amount of sun-dappled Saturday nonchalance to 312. The outer door was open. I checked the mailboxes. There were names in all the slots but one. None of them said C. F. Congdon or just Congdon. Or, Condon, for that matter. I looked at the building directory. All but one of the apartments—1F, 1R, et cetera—had a name next to it, all matching the mailbox names. The one lacking a name was 2F.

Since no one answering to the applicable description went out or came in, it felt safe to return to the car unnoticed. There was the possibility that if Conor Condon happened to be gazing out of his window to gauge the weather or whatever, he could see me leaving. I assumed it wouldn't mean much to him.

"Yeah?" Izzy Abramovitz said as I opened the car door. I told him what I'd seen. Make that what I hadn't seen. "That tells me—us—one of two things, maybe three things. One, the apartment is empty. He counted on his stubby fingers. Two, someone is livin' there who doesn't want it known but who ain't our man. Three, Condon is livin' there and, like all criminals, doesn't want it known. There is a fourth possibility—someone is livin' there who hasn't gotten around to addin' his or her name or their names. I'm gonna rule that out. I'm gonna rule out number one and two, too, and go with three. We're gonna assume 2F is Condon's little hideaway and keep watchin'. If it takes all day. You're gonna ask me what we do if we see him come out of the buildin'. I'm not answerin' that just yet. Right now, it's for me to know and you to find out."

"Just let me confirm," I said, "that according to Ms. Belfer, Conor Condon never put his name on his mailbox downtown or had it added to the directory, either."

"There you go," Izzy Abramovitz said, "Ms. Belfer can be good for somethin'."

We sat. Izzy Abramovitz gripped the wheel. Once in a while, he removed his right hand and drummed his fingers on the dashboard. He turned the radio on once, pushed buttons to find a station he liked, gave it less than a minute, snapped it off. "All you get these days is junk. Rap music. Do you know what they're goin' on about?" I didn't answer. "I don't. They're not in love with cops. I can tell that much."

I thought about what I might say but couldn't think of anything to which he wouldn't take objection. That's how we remained for an hour or so, always keeping our eyes on 312.

When Izzy Abramovitz took his eyes off 312 for a second, he said to me, "You know, kid, you never did tell me how you got on to this Cutler thing." He returned to watching 312. "Why don't you tell me now? We got nothin' better to do. I'm innerested."

The couple times he'd asked me before, I'd skirted around it. Then, the subject changed fast enough for me to keep my hallucinatory, potentially institution-committing answer to myself. But now? He'd asked outright when there was nothing but time to kill. I toyed with telling the truth, but only toyed. I suppose that to satisfy him I could dream something up about meeting somebody somewhere, but I couldn't kid myself that was going to appease Izzy Abramovitz.

My stalling, brief as it was, wasn't sitting well with him. "Come on, boychik, come on," he was saying when a figurative bell in the shape of a uniformed figure saved me.

"Well, look at that," Izzy Abramovitz suddenly said. "If it ain't the postman. Excu-uuse me, the post*wo*man. I think I'll have a little talk with 'er. "

With one hand he opened his door. With the other he applied the Binaca. Funny, Izzy Abramovitz had never Binaca-ed for me. Maybe he had before he arrived for any of our confabs. I thought I'd never know unless I asked him outright. Not.

"I'll see to this," he said. "You stay here and keep your eye on 312." He slammed the door shut. The postwoman was pushing her bag in from Broadway on the north side of the street. I watched Izzy Abramovitz long enough to see that as he approached her, he pulled out something I took to be a shield. But not his old shield. From somewhere in my memory stacks, I retrieved the fact that on retirement policemen and policewomen are required to turn in their shields. Izzy Abramovitz must have flashed a fake shield. Who knows what? I suppose that could get him in trouble for impersonating a policeman, but no, not slippery Izzy Abramovitz.

I got back to scrutinizing 312.

Full disclosure: When I saw Izzy Abramovitz flash whatever he was flashing, I thought he was showing a badge. When he was back in the car, I asked about the badge. He said, "That wasn't a badge, boy-o. That was a shield. A shield. You got that?" I stood—or sat—corrected. "Not a police shield, by the way. I turned that in when I retired. What I flashed was a Captain Midnight badge— not a shield—I had when I was a kid. You never know when somethin' like that'll be useful."

Landing back in the Honda Civic so heavily that it rocked, Izzy Abramovitz concluded his shield lecture and said, "Okay, I found out what I—what we—want to know. I asked postwoman Williams what she knows about 312, whether she's been delivering mail to anyone name of Congdon or Condon, first name maybe Conor. She said in the last year—she's only had this route for a year, give or take—she delivered maybe a half dozen letters and a few bigger manila envelopes addressed to the Congdon name.

"At first, she didn't see the name on any of the boxes, but she did what they do. She left the first couple letters on top of the boxes. Like they do in case somebody in the buildin' knows anything. The letters disappeared, never stayed where she left 'em, never were marked anythin' like "return to sender" or "not at this address." She decided the mailbox with no name had to belong to Congdon and started puttin' mail in the box. It never stayed there. Nothing backin' up, except once or twice for a few days, then empty again. She figured vacation or some reason to be out of town."

He clapped his fat hands together. "We got our man. Can you beat that?"

I wanted to clap, too, but didn't. I wasn't certain I was at liberty to do it. Even with this latest development, I still didn't know how I stood with him. I said a blunt, "Now what?"

"I'll tell you 'now what.' First off, I asked her if she ever saw a man goin' in or out of the buildin' answerin' to your description. She said she couldn't be sure. She said she sees a lot of people goin' in and outta buildins. Maybe she did."

He gave me another helping of his eye-popping jeepers-creepers treatment. "And now I'm gonna tell you more 'now what.' On the assumption that this Conor Condon character lives at 312, we're gonna play by his rules and con him. We're gonna con the conman. Me and you, boychik, me and you."

We're still watching 312, not each other. As he's beginning to lay this out, I couldn't see his expression. I couldn't see mine, either, but I must have looked apprehensive. I didn't know where this was going, but I understood enough about Izzy Abramovitz to know there was little he'd stop at.

He did stop. "Hold it," he said. "Look what's over there."

I saw what he saw, but because I was concentrating on his incipient plan, I hadn't registered it. A tall, bulky, graying blond man had exited 312. He had the look and the walk of a former quarterback who hadn't entirely kept his youthful frame intact but was still something of a bruiser.

I knew in my bones what Izzy Abramovitz knew. (Whatever that means; what do bones know that the brain doesn't?) I knew this was Con Condon in the middle-age flesh, not Amy Pritchard, not George Reiser. This was Conor Condon—aka C. F. Congdon—crossing the street and angling toward the Honda Civic 2008 model.

I said, "It's Conor Condon, isn't it?"

"It ain't his brother."

"Why is he heading this way?"

"That's what I'd like to know. I don't think he spotted us. I never saw him at his window."

Con Conor was now about twenty feet from the Honda Civic and walking rapidly toward us, walking athletically and substantiating what I knew of his background.

"Here's what we do," Izzy Abramovitz said. "We talk to each other like two people just parked on the street. That way I'm facin' you and won't see 'im, and he won't see my face. But you'll see 'im." He turned to me, put on what passed for an Izzy Abramovitz smile. "Don't look right at him. Keep facin' me. Thaaat's right. Just get 'im in your peripheral vision. This is all bein' cautious. If he's suspicious. He may not be."

We were finding out. Izzy Abramovitz said the last two or three sentences through his smile. I listened and threw in a laugh of my own, turning my head as you do, only briefly taking Con Condon in. He had the looks of a man in his forties who had been handsome when young, was still handsome and trim but less handsome without having gone to seed.

He was wearing a blue polo shirt, khaki trousers and a pair of overdesigned, multicolored running shoes. (Spanking new Adidas?) I took in a determined gaze and mouth held taut, as if he was thinking some sneaky thought. I have to concede I might be concocting the sneaky part. He passed the Honda Civic without paying any noticeable attention to us. He kept up the athletic gait.

"Where is he now?" Izzy Abramovitz wanted to know. We were still facing each other. He'd dumped the grin.

So had I. I said, "Still walking down the street. He never looked in the car."

"That don't mean he didn't take us in. That's okay. Matter of fact, it plays right into my plan. Here's what we're gonna do. Listen up. A lot of it is gonna fall on you, boychik. If Conor is on to us or even if he ain't, we're gonna force him to give himself up."

He paused slightly. The piercing eyes narrowed.

What was I in for?

"We have his phone number. That drivin' incident record. It's a cell phone exchange. He prob'ly doesn't have a landline. His kind never does. So what you're gonna do is phone him. When he picks up, you're gonna say, 'We know what you did.' Maybe he'll say something like 'Who's this?' or 'Oh, yeah, what did I do?' Maybe he'll say nothing. You give him a couple seconds. You say nothing. You hang up.

"Now I think about it, don't say, 'We know what you did.' Say, 'I know what you did.' That way he thinks there's only one person doin' this. If he noticed two people in the car, he may not connect that with the call. You got it so far?"

Yes, I got it. I got that Con Condon could identify my number. That could be bad enough. What if his guilt kicked in? What if he got vengeful, got devious—a guy of his height and girth?

"You think I'm askin' you to call from your phone. No, boychik. You're gonna call from mine. It's untraceable."

He wrangled his cell phone from the inside breast pocket of his shapeless jacket. "Yeah, you're gonna phone from mine. Not once, but twice. You get it? I been givin' this some thought. You hafta trust me. I know, Daniel Freund, when people say, 'Trust me,' that's the first sign you better not trust 'em. But you can trust me. Got it?"

I nodded. Despite everything—or despite much of it—I had worked this out: Izzy Abramovitz was so brusquely honest he was too sold on himself not to be trustworthy.

He was waiting for me to answer. "I got it."

"You ready for this?"

"As I'll ever be," I said, which meant I might never be ready, but I'd have to go through with it for Izzy Abramovitz's trustworthy plan to have an effect.

"All right, let me explain what I'm up to. You call him again." He pointed at his phone, which I was now holding. "This time you say, 'I know what you did three years ago to make certain you get all that Dayton money.' If he tries to interrupt, you say, 'I'm doin' the talkin' here, and I want to know why you think you should keep all that cash for yourself. I think you oughta divvy it up, spread it around. Like to me.'

"If he tries to innerrupt, you say, 'It's bad manners to innerrupt.' You say, 'Sure, you don't have to cut me in on what's left, a big slice of what's left. I'm just as happy to let the New York police and the Dayton police know what I know. So whaddaya say?' You say, 'You got five seconds. Five, four, three—.' I'll be a monkey's uncle if he don't stop you and say somethin' like he doesn't know what the fuck you're talkin' about—denial ain't just a river in Egypt—but he's agreeable to meet you and straighten things out. You say okay to that and suggest a neutral place. Someplace like Central Park or Riverside Park.

"That's up to you. He's not gonna go for it. He's gonna want some place he's got more control, some place he can take things into his hands. His apartment. You stall for a couple seconds. You're thinkin' it over. Then you say, 'Okay, but it's gotta be soon. Don't think you're gonna drag this out or run out on me.'"

He stopped for a second. "You got all that?"

Yes, I got all that, and I'm thinking about being alone with this gonzo killer and the creepy old saw about once you kill, the next time is easier. Then a worse thought twitches my stricken brain. It's something that struck me when I was going through the Dayton obituaries. It's the three or four, maybe five times the cause of death wasn't specified. Maybe they were also murders passing as poisonings or, uh, suicides.

Izzy Abramovitz picked up on the hesitation. "Whatsa matter, boy? Not gettin' cold feet after you done so much work, are you?"

"No," I stammered. We both knew I was lying. "It does sound dangerous."

"Maybe if anyone else was puttin' this together. Not when Izzy Abramovitz has your back. Maybe you're thinkin' all this sounds like entrapment. You got that right, boychik. It is, but so what? So what the fuck what? Wake up, kid, it's the twenty-first century. And I'm no longer on the police force."

To set my obviously rattled mind at ease, he applied the Izzy Abramovitz signature snirk, i.e., a sneer-smirk mashup. My mind wasn't eased, but saying that to him would accomplish nothing. I applied the signature apprehensive Daniel Freund smile I'd undoubtedly been applying for much of the past twenty-four hours. My friends would recognize it.

"Now all we do is wait for a good time to make the calls," Izzy Abramovitz said. "Which prob'ly ain't now. We need to catch him at home. Look around to see if you see him coming."

We looked. No sign of Con Condon in any direction.

"Nope," Izzy Abramovitz picked up. "If he did catch us here before, we don't want 'im catchin' us here again." He turned the key in the ignition and started backing out. He did it with the ease of a Nascar champ. "We get outta here, go back to your house and wait. Maybe we give him a few hours. Whaddaya say we grab some lunch? Your treat."

Off we went. Izzy Abramovitz found his downtown parking space with no problem, natch, near Ben's, the hole-in-the-wall kosher deli on West Thirty-eighth Street. We left the Honda Civic 2008 model. As we did, I noticed he had been sitting—for years, I assumed, maybe at least a decade—on a worn seat cushion. Peeking out at its edges was fraying gray Honda Civic upholstery.

When we sidled into nothing like up-to-date seats at a cramped Ben's table and accustomed ourselves—I mean didn't accustom ourselves—to the ambient kosher-type noise, he didn't ask, as some people might have, what kind of food I liked. He waved menus away. He knew what he liked and, since he wasn't paying, I didn't argue with him. What would have been the point? I was to have no say.

I was to have what he had, and what he had was a pastrami sandwich and seltzer. This was ordered from Shimon, perhaps the last surviving Jewish deli waiter in the entire city, maybe the entire state. Shimon seemed to know Izzy Abramovitz—or at least gave him a big "Velcome beck, lung time, no see" greeting.

Izzy Abramovitz instructed, "Don't go light on the pastrami."

Shimon came back, as if they were doing a Weber and Fields routine, with, "Duntchoo tink I know to whom I'm addressink?"

Izzy Abramovitz was civil through the lunch. That is, he was civil to the extent he could be. I won't go into his eating habits, other than to say gusto doesn't do justice to the way he attacked his food. Nor was talking while chewing beyond him.

Before and after we—he—ordered, before and after Shimon brought the orders to our cramped table, looking as if he might collapse at any moment, Izzy Abramovitz repeated the Con Conor particulars as far as they'd gone. He had me parrot them back again and again.

He couldn't miss my palpable trepidation. When he satisfied himself that I knew those particulars inside out, he admitted that there was no predicting precisely what would transpire when I was alone with Conor Condon.

I fixed tremblingly on what happens to supposedly superior invading forces when the enemy is on his own territory. I didn't say as much but continued nodding my head in fake compliance.

I admit I considered pulling out, but I remembered

what I'd chosen to do. If I even tried to run like hell in
the opposite direction, what were the chances that a disembodied hand—joined by an ethereal chorus of *Great
Gatsby* East Eggers—might reach out over a great distance and pummel me in the solar plexus?

The thing to do was listen to Izzy Abramovitz and
believe him. He was an experienced police detective. He
must have been in similar situations before, likely many
times. Similar but not the same—not exactly entrapment,
you know. But well, maybe. Why else would he have produced his plan so thoroughly?

I was deciding I'd try to reassure him that I was reas-
sured, when, whether he would believe me or not, he
changed the subject. He may have meant merely to dis-
tract me, but he said, "Boychik, you still ain't told me how
you got all tied up in this thin'."

I still hadn't hit on a version more acceptable than the
real (the surreal?) one. Nevertheless, a made-up tale it
would have to be. And it would have to be now. There
wasn't much hope of a blessed interruption. We were still
working on our foot-high pastrami, and he had already
ordered halvah for dessert.

Since truth is stranger than fiction—it undeniably was
in my instance—I settled on conjuring up a bland fiction
that Izzy Abramovitz might settle for. With as little hesitation or questionable frills that I could conjure, I said,

"You know how neighborhoods are. There are always rumors floating around. I don't even remember which neighbor I ran into—not Ms. Belfer—who brought up the subject of the building where there'd been a murder the police thought was a suicide. It was another neighbor who said which building. I became intrigued. I guess you could say that's why we're here today."

Izzy Abramovitz gave me those accusatory blinkers. He said, "That's your story, and you're stickin' to it. But not for long, if I have anythin' to say about it." He was wiping his mouth and rising. He threw his napkin on the table as if in defiance of what I'd told him. "It's time to make those calls. I'll take the halvah with me. Let's go."

I paid the bill, and we were out of Ben's and into the Honda Civic, where he took a swig of the (stale?) Coors before turning the ignition key.

We were on the way to my building. There, Izzy Abramovitz's talent for homing in on parking spaces didn't fail him. Turning off the ignition, he said, "Okay, Daniel Freund, time to get down to cases."

He pulled out his cell phone from the same suit pocket and handed it to me. He pulled another note from a different pocket. "I'll read the phone number. You dial."

He did as announced. I did as trained.

Conor Condon picked up the phone on the first ring and said with no patience, "What do you want?" His tone suggested he was someone who liked to do the phoning, not the other way around.

I looked at Izzy Abramovitz, who recognized I'd connected and nodded a stern go-ahead. With as much testosterone as I could summon, I said, "I know what you did," then ended the call halfway through Con Condon's resonantly baritone "Who's thi—?"

Izzy Abramovitz nodded approval and said, "We wait five minutes. This is workin' just like I said." We sat in silence. He never looked at his watch. He was on top of the time just as he was on top of everything else. Or so he let you know without saying so.

I summoned the testosterone again, called again and delivered the lines I'd learned, including the one about not brooking interruptions. Playing my part, I was impressed by how closely Con Conor rendered his foretold responses.

While listening, I occasionally looked at Izzy Abramovitz, who wasn't looking at me. He was listening to my side of the conversation with his head and virtually nonexistent neck bent over and his hands gripping the Honda Civic 2008 model wheel.

Our charged tête-à-tête ended without Con Conor learning anything about me or, more vitally, Izzy Abramovitz's and my scheme. I dodged every one of his leading queries. We hung up after he agreed to setting a one o'clock afternoon meeting the next day at his 312, 2F apartment.

He wasn't putting me off, nor was he hurrying the up-close-and-personal. I thought the nearly twenty-four-hour delay might have been chosen so he could devise something in his favor, some revolting scheme to put me at a disadvantage. But Izzy Abramovitz could hear what I was outlining. He nodded assent to everything he heard.

The conversation over, I handed the cell phone back. "You did good," Izzy Abramovitz said. He had the effrontery to pat me on the head.

I asked, "What do you make of his not agreeing to meet me until tomorrow at one o'clock when I suggested earlier?"

"I like it. He's already thinkin' he's got the upper hand. Just the corner I want to push him into. This way, when he sees you, he'll think he's gonna gain that much more of an advantage over you."

I threw my hands up. It was an instantaneous gesture. I couldn't stop myself.

"Don't get your bowels in an uproar. You saw him. He's still got the look of a high school jerk who knows how to zigzag down the field for a seventy-five-yard touchdown. You look like what you look like. A hundred seventy pounds, or close enough, of a onetime college flake. No offense."

I took it as an offense but kept it to myself.

"That's what we want. He'll be off-balance just when he thinks he's got the upper hand. All you have to remember is I got your back. Your front, too, boychik. Now get out of the car and get ready for tomorrow. I'll pick you up at 12:15."

I did, without saying goodbye. I was too preoccupied thinking about how I was going to get through the next however-many hours. I also wondered why he was picking me up at 12:15 for a one o'clock appointment. A last-minute pep talk?

Again, I gave part of the rest of the day and evening over to making phone calls to friends. I hoped they would get my mind off things. They didn't. Just about everyone asked what I'd been doing the past few days. What could I tell them? That I'd been solving a murder that had once been designated a suicide? They all knew I liked a good kibbitz, but they weren't going to go for that one, certainly not if I tacked on that my investigation had been instigated by none other than the late literary giant F. Scott Fitzgerald.

Most of them knew my attitude toward Fitzgerald and *The Great Gatsby,* but they would, could, regard this wacky claim as more than a kibbutz, more likely as a symptom of something worrying. So, remaining the inured liar, I told them I'd gotten an idea for a new story and had immersed myself in it.

They'd all heard about my writer's block *ad nauseum* and so congratulated me and encouraged me to go for it. "What's it about?" was the general response. I said, with the novelist's generic rejoinder, "I'm not saying just yet. I don't want to talk so much about it that I talk it out."

Before I fell into a restless sleep—no dreams survived—I bucked myself up. Or tried to. I emphasized the F. Scott Fitzgerald/*Great Gatsby* motif. I had been chosen by my favorite novel and, by effortless extension, by Fitzgerald himself to take on the delicate, dangerous job of finding a murderer and bringing him to justice.

Lord, what fools us mortals be.

SUNDAY

Breakfast was no less restless than the wee hours had been, but tense as I was, I was relieved when at 12:13 I saw the Honda Civic 2008 model heading my way, stopping in front of the building. As I went to the car, I waved to omnipresent Ms. Belfer.

I said "Good morning" to Izzy Abramovitz, shut the car door and inserted the seatbelt catch.

"It better be a good morning," he said and pulled away, turned left up Eighth Avenue, stopped at the next light, turned left again and slipped into a parking space.

When he stopped the car, he said, "Just to make sure it's as good as can be, we need to take precautions." He reached over his seat and grabbed something from the conglomeration of objects on the back seat. "We're goin' to wire you up."

What!

"Don't get alarmed. There's nothin' to it, and how else do you think we get a record of the full confession you're gonna wheedle out of the Con guy?"

He was making the kind of sense I wanted to hear nothing of.

"Wired?" I said with terror in my tone.

"That's what I said, boychik. Some people think it's old hat, but that's some people wedded to more advanced technology. Get your shirt off." I was wearing a cotton blazer, a white shirt, and, for supportive pizzazz, solid-yellow tie. "Come on, boy-o, no time to waste."

I disrobed. What would passersby think is going on?

Izzy Abramovitz anticipated me. "Don't worry about what people think. Only fools worry about what other people think. That's my philosophy. You didn't think I had one, didya?"

As he spoke. he was continuing to outfit me.

"What if Con Conor checks me for a wire?"

"He won't. He thinks you're showing up to extort money from him. Why would he think you'd be wearing a wire that could incriminate both of you?"

"How about if he notices it under my shirt?"

"He won't. For one thing, you'll button your coat. And the tie'll obscure it."

"What if he tells me to unbutton my coat and relax?"

"You'll unbutton it. Stop the pussyfootin'. You're the one wanted to solve this murder."

Again, Izzy Abramovitz was making the sort of sense I didn't want him to make. He finished his work, patted my chest, said, "It looks great, even if I have to say so myself. I didn't think I'd be rusty."

He readjusted himself on his mistreated seat cushion and started the car. He and scared-silly me were on
our way to 312. As usual and to my mounting chagrin, he
made good time. He repeated his instructions more than
once—and then once again after he'd parked some five or
so minutes early.

Not on Conor Condon's block. So that were the Conman looking out any of his three windows, he wouldn't
recognize the Honda Civic 2008 model as having been
the same Honda Civic 2008 model parked on the street
the day before.

We agreed I'd buzz the fall guy at precisely one o'clock.
Izzy Abramovitz's reasoning: If I arrived too early, I'd
seem anxious. If I arrived late, I could give the impression I was evincing overconfidence. Arriving on the busi-
ness-like dot could imply I meant business but possibly
was too carefully conscientious.

Zero hour arrived. Actually, zero hour minus one. I
left the Honda Civic Model 2008 at 12:58. And, knowing
Izzy Abramovitz was watching me, walked with my idea
of purpose. As I rounded the corner and could no longer
be watched, I worked at keeping up the purpose. I also
remained aware of the wire, which was light but still felt
as if it was burning a cavernous hole in my chest.

I reached 312 West Eighty-eighth at the agreed-on
time. I went through the open outer door. I pushed the

right button on the directory, the one next to the vacant slot. I waited. I waited. I waited. I waited as much as a minute. I debated buzzing again but didn't. Nor did I tap my toes. I understood what was going on. Con Conor was making me wait. He was immediately employing the get-the-upper-hand tactic.

I waited, I'd say, another ten seconds, when the entry buzzed kicked in. I heard, "2F." Nothing else. I mounted the stairs to the second floor, remarking to myself that I wasn't quaking. I couldn't afford to quake. A quaking fig-ure wasn't going to get anything out of Con Conor.

When I reached the second floor and swiveled, the door directly in front of me opened. Con Condon stepped out, said "Conor Condon." He offered his hand and added, "Your name?"

I suppressed the ingrained reflex to shake and said, "My name isn't important. You know what I'm here for."

Con Conor retracted his hand, turning the gesture into an invite to enter the apartment. Before I accepted the offer, I took in all six foot three (?) of him. He was dressed as he'd been the day before, not the same clothes but similar.

I got a better look at his face—the distrustful ice-green eyes, the mended nose (a football field run-in?), the cyn-ic's mouth. I saw up close the maturing quarterback phy-sique not so aged that it had lost its innate power. I was close enough to take in heavy cologne. I've never known enough about cologne to identify individual scents, but this one was the kind men slap on to impress women who, they think, fall for that kind of thing.

I hesitated long enough for Con Conor to see what I was doing. Only then did I follow the gesturing arm, the polo shirt revealing a taut biceps, years of hurling a football still holding up.

I entered a living room furnished like an airline hospitality suite. It was modern in an impersonal way. It said, Make yourself comfortable but not with any thought of staying long.

Pointing at a sofa faced into the room and positioned three or four feet away from the front windows, he said, "You say I know what you're here for. I don't."

He was waiting for me to sit on the sofa. I remembered the old Mafia rule about never facing away from a window. I'd started to the sofa but stopped. I noticed two Eero Saarinen chairs opposite the sofa at an angle to each other—as Saarinen never intended them to be angled. They faced the windows. I said, "They look good." I went to one and sat down. Con Conor, showing no questioning response to my choice, took the other one. He had to angle it more directly toward me.

I said, "You know why I'm here, but if you need reminding, I'm more than glad to do it."

"I know you said you know what I did."

"I said more than that. I said I know what you did and why you did it. You had your eye on the money, the tontine money."

"The *what* money?" He stood up. Until then, I was congratulating myself on how well I was doing. I was also hoping the wire was transmitting properly and that Izzy Abramovitz, if not pleased, was sufficiently satisfied with my introductory remarks.

But when Con Conor stood, I may have flinched. I hoped that if I had, it was imperceptible.

It may not have been. Con Condon's mouth tightened. One side lowered. I thought I saw light enter his eyes. He said with what I'll call an incipient leer. "I'm going to mix myself a drink. Can I get you one? Whatever you want. I'm fully stocked."

"No thanks," I said, no vocal tremor yet. "I'm not here to drink." I recalled the skinny I'd heard about his drinking.

"I'm sorry," he said, as he went to a bar he'd set up at the east wall of the living room. He went behind it and apparently opened a small refrigerator door. He set an ice tray atop the bar, again reached under and lifted a bottle of Dewar's scotch and a bottle of Schweppes Club Soda. He took his time mixing the drink.

From where he was standing on the other side of the

bar, he said, "Go on. You can continue." He was extracting ice cubes from the tray. "Are you sure you don't want a drink while I'm here? Maybe something soft? Diet Coke?"

At the same time the "Diet Coke?" was said to insult my manliness, he was playing the perfect host. I guess the Condons were a devoted cocktails family. I shook my head no and perhaps succeeded at affecting annoyance.

"You were saying?" he said. Then, for no reason at all, or because he had a definite reason, he picked up an outsize corkscrew and twirled it around. After a couple of twirls, I'd say, to establish that it could serve as a weapon, he set it down and returned to his Eero Saarinen.

I acted as if his actions were nothing out of the ordinary. To a casual observer, they wouldn't have been.

I was feeling nowhere near casual but said, as he returned "Look, Con Condon, I don't want to waste your time, and I'm damned if you're going to waste mine." I hoped that transmitted theatrically well. "I'll cut to the chase."

"Oh, there's a chase underway?" he said, planting both feet on the geometrically patterned rug under our feet.

I ignored the snide undertone and said, "Three years ago, when you were living downtown on the ground floor in a building and were directly under Fulton Cutler—."

"Fulton who?"

"Fulton Cutler," I said at a deliberately slow tempo. "The name isn't new to you. Three years ago on a warm spring night, you came into your garden, placed a ladder you'd stored against the back wall, climbed through the open window into Fulton Cutler's study, startled Fulton Cutler quickly enough to fire the Magnum .38 you held in one gloved hand, bent the dead man over his desk, pressed his right hand around the grip and let it fall.

"Then you opened the knapsack or bag you carried in over your shoulder and took out an envelope or box containing a suicide note—." I put "suicide note" in air quotes. "— and placed it on the desk, where nobody could miss seeing it. Maybe it was then you looked at the study door, saw it was shut and noticed the key. You went over to lock it, pocketed the key and congratulated yourself for creating the appearance of a locked room.

"Next, you went back to the knapsack to get out the tub of Flex Seal and a brush you also brought along, swabbed down the bottom of the window frame and the length of wood it closes on. That was all you had to do. Maybe because you thought you heard a sound from inside the building or some other kind of disturbance, you threw everything back into the knapsack, climbed out the window taking care not to get any of the Flex Seal on you, yanked the window down so that the Flex Seal would adhere.

"My guess is you didn't miss the Flex Seal container, the Flex Seal tub, until you got back downstairs, into your apartment, opened the bag and realized it wasn't there. It was too late to climb back up. That would have meant getting the ladder from where you replaced it at the bottom of the garden. Worse, you knew you wouldn't be able to pry the window open. By then the Flex Seal would have done its business. But you were wearing gloves, and so you knew no fingerprints would be on the container. You patted yourself on the back for carrying out the perfect murder, even more perfect with the locked study door."

I stopped to see what Con Conor was making of this. I'd given my Izzy Abramovitz-drilled speech—much of which I expanded on as I was talking—as if I were a character in a play. I think that's how I got through it. Any other way I would have been too disoriented.

"Great story," Con Conor said, taking a very long swig of scotch, "but ridiculous. Ludicrous."

Even in my high-anxiety state I mused that guilty figures caught red-handed in detective fiction always sputter "ridiculous" and "ludicrous." Here was Conman Condon doing it in real life, as if to prove yet again that life imitates art.

Acting the cool customer, Con Conor did his own musing. "Why would I want to get rid of an upstairs neighbor I'd never even seen in a building I never lived in? Because he made too much noise when he walked around and should've put down thicker rugs?" He indulged in another one of his leers. "Tell me another one."

"I don't have to tell you another one," I said with what was passing for my modicum of confidence. "I'll continue this one. You may never have met Fulton Cutler, but you knew who he was. Matter of fact, you may have met him at some point in your Dayton, Ohio, boyhood."

"Dayton? When was I ever in Dayton, Ohio?"

"From birth on, until you left for college and law school, dropped out and started bumming around. You only returned to Dayton from time to time, the last time when you took the money and, like they say, ran."

In an inexplicable way, I was beginning to catch the spirit of the thing. I was infused with the fun of improv. "You know exactly what I'm talking about. The tontine money."

"Tontine money. What's tontine money?"

"I'm not going to dignify that with an answer. You took the tontine money." I pointed around the room. I indicated the Eero Saarinen chairs. "You're living on it now. I've got you where I want you."

I embarrassed myself with the "I've-got-you-where-I want-you cliché but forget that. By now I'd pulled out all the stops. "I'd like to be living like this myself. I know you have enough to split the rest with me. If not, I go to the police with what I know. You wouldn't be too happy if the police heard the mouthful I can tell them about you and your activities. You'd like to head that off, even at a cost to your bank account. That's why I'm here. That's why you asked me here."

"You're making a big mistake, buddy," Con Conor said with his pleased-as-scotch-and-soda grin, his legs now crossed at the ankles and stretched out in front of him. "How would I know about any of this? Looks like it's time for you to go."

While I was thinking how I was going to leave without getting his confession, he stood, still cucumber cool.

Thinking fast, I said, "While you were busy doing your dirty deed, you might have noticed the scrapbook on the desk and the *Dayton Daily News* by it. You would have done yourself a favor if you'd opened it up, but you were in too much of a hurry to shoot and split."

Where was all this coming from? Damned if I know: a glowing book on an end table? "If you'd given yourself another couple of minutes, you'd have found out that the only clippings in the scrapbook were obituaries of seventeen Fifth Street Fraternity members. If you'd opened the hometown newspaper, the *Dayton Daily News*, on the desk next to the scrapbook, you would have realized that what Fulton Cutler was about to paste into the scrapbook was the obituary of the eighteenth member.

"That left only Fulton Cutler and your father waiting to collect the tontine prize. Let's just say if money is the motive behind nine-and-a-half out of ten murders, you've got the money motive. You know you're your father's heir, even if you think daddy Conrad Condon fouled up your life. This is your way, among other things, to get the last laugh on him."

Conor Condon sat down. He quaffed the remaining scotch in one fierce gulp. He said, "My dad, the old bastard."

That was my opening. "Did I just hear a confession?" Did Izzy Abramovitz just hear a confession?

Conor Condon stood up, the empty glass in his right hand. He started circling the room. "He owed me the money after fucking up my life. I could've been in the NFL. Instead, I go to law school. I never wanted to go to fucking law school. I didn't even last the first year. Constitutional Law. Give me a break. He didn't deserve to live. No, he deserved to live until he became the last surviving Fifth Street Fraternity asshole. Then he deserved to die. I would have helped him along then, too, but I got lucky. He was already dying. Cancer. Cancer of the soul, I call it."

Con Conor was behind the bar, mixing himself another scotch and soda. He was also thinking. He started laughing, the laugh Lucifer might let fly when confronting a conniving fool in need.

"You think you have some kind of goods on me. You

have nothing, not a damn thing. From what you've told me, you have nothing but circumstantial evidence. And what about the suicide note? In Cutler's handwriting, on Cutler's stationery?"

I had to admit that was a baffler, but I tried not to look baffled, only unfazed.

Con Conor pressed on, his hands gripping the bar, leaning forward in triumph. "That note was what gave me the whole idea. I found it on my father's desk. Just lying there. It wasn't a suicide note at all. 'I've had enough of this.' You know what he had enough of? The whole tontine business. That's the big joke of it. All the members had been back and forth and back and forth over it as their numbers dwindled. All those prominent citizens, all those pillars of the community. They were such assholes over their stupid secret society. They never knew what jokes they were to the rest of us. Fulton Cutler was sick of hearing about it."

Talk about being wired up. Con Conor was the poster boy.

"And there it was, that note. I'd gone into the old man's study to go through his desk drawers on one of my visits home, looking for cash. He always had some handy. I saw the note and pocketed it. Then I pocketed some cash. I doubt he ever missed the money or the note. He was so out of it most of the time.

"I'd been trying to think of some way to make sure he was the last survivor, and there was that piece of paper. That's what got me to take that vacant apartment under Cutler. His return address was on the envelope. I came to New York with the note, figuring I'd find someplace near him. I could watch him, get the drop on him. When I found I could be in the same building, I knew I was on the right track. Everything fell into place. I knew how I'd be able to put the note to good use. When you get lucky like that, you know what you're doing is what you're supposed to be doing."

I was still wearing the telltale wire, and Conor Condon had just laid it all out.

I said, "Believable suicide note or not, I bet you think there's only circumstantial evidence, and circumstantial evidence isn't enough to get authorities to dust off the case. You think some prosecutor wouldn't love to get his—or her—hands on this one?"

Still behind the bar, Con leaned over and let go with another steely look directly handed down from Lucifer. Or is it up?

"You think you're pretty smart," he simmered. "You're not. You know the one where the guy says, 'I could tell you all about it, but if I do, I have to kill you'? Right about now it looks like I already told you all about it. So—."

He put down the empty glass, and from one of the

bar shelves concealed from me, produced a revolver. I guessed it was a Magnum .38. That Magnum .38? Was he partial to those, maybe for sentimental reasons?

He went on. "So, if I've already told you, it looks like I have to kill you."

I'm reporting this calmly now. I think they call it sangfroid, but my sang was the farthest thing from froid. Not to put too fine a point on it, I was scared shitless. This isn't what I'd signed up for when F. Scott Fitzgerald's prose started effervescing, started fulminating.

What I found to say scared me worse. "What if you do? What makes you think I haven't told anyone else? I could have someone outside waiting for me."

The .38 still pointed at me, Conman Condon came around the bar, looked me over. (Why couldn't Izzy Abramovitz have outfitted me with a bulletproof vest instead of a wire? Or better yet, both.) He said, "Wait just a minute. I thought you looked familiar. You were sitting in a car across the street yesterday. I knew there was something funny about it."

"That was me." Then I did something you're not supposed to do when you're wearing a wire. I'd already unbuttoned my jacket. Now I flipped my tie aside and unbuttoned my shirt. "And the other guy is at the other end of this wire."

"You fucking creep," Con Condon said and started

toward me, the .38 pointed not at my heart but at the wire.

Then simultaneously, two things occurred: (1) There was a banging on Con Condon's apartment door and "Open up. Police."; and (2) Con Condon hurtled toward me but stumbled on the one-yard line. I assume it was the scotch and sodas taking potent effect. His left sneaker caught under the rug.

(Could be with that gift for fumbling he wouldn't have become such an NFL superstar, after all.)

As he fell, his packing right hand angled way up, the .38 fired, the bullet hitting the ceiling and the revolver sailing out of his hand.

In my direction. I grabbed it with no idea what I would do with it. Not so. I did know enough to point it at the Conman, who was still on his hospitality-suite floor, where only seconds before he'd been offering an unusual type of hospitality.

Was there even another bullet in the revolver? I had no idea. What did I know from Magnum .38s?

I had him in my sights just as the police broke through the door. There were four or five of them with firearms drawn. Among them was Izzy Abramovitz, who came over to me and skillfully grabbed the firearm I was awkwardly packing. He also took me by the shoulder to keep me from toppling.

The police, a few of them from the group I'd encountered at the Tenth Precinct, handcuffed the revealed Conman and escorted him from the building past several people who'd collected to see what was going on.

Izzy Abramovitz led me from the building. He got me
around the corner and into the Honda Civic 2008 model.
He did his seatbelt and helped me with mine. He abandoned the parking space with his usual aplomb.

As he did, he spoke, keeping his eyes on the road. "I
have somethin' to explain, and I don't like dealin' in expla-
nations. But you deserve it. It's about the police. I couldn't
tell you I contacted Doyle, who believed your story when
it came from me. I didn't wanna let you know what was
up. I didn't want you goin' in there too confident. Conor
might have smelled it out. Long as he thought he had the
drop on you, he was gonna talk more freely. And he did.
You got 'im goin', boychik. I gotta hand it to you. I'd say
we made a great team, 'cept I never work in teams if I can
avoid it. Not since that nitwit Dugan."

He didn't say much more on the way downtown. He
did pat me on the knee, patting still an Izzy Abramovitz
stratagem to keep me in my place. When he stopped in
front of my building, he said, "You may have to give your
side of what went on in a day or two. Or not. In the meantime, get some rest."

He reached across me with his heavy arm and opened

the door. As I got out, almost stable in my footing, he said, "I told you I had your back. I told you I'd call in other cops when the time was right. I told you I know how to close a case in no time flat. Now I've closed this one twice in no time flat."

How about his appropriating total success in the reopened-and-shut case? There are several responses I might have made. I didn't make any. I finished shutting the Honda Civic 2008 model door.

But the second before I did, he wedged in, "Make sure you give my regards to Ms. Belfer. And one last thin'. Someday you're gonna tell me the real story of how you got goin' on all this."

That was all. Izzy Abramovitz pulled away without looking back.

I climbed the stoop, gave the requested regards to Ms. Belfer from my stoop to hers and went to my apartment.

I had only one aim in mind. To hear what *The Great Gatsby* Hal Siegel 1953 edition had to say. I fixed it with my idea of a basilisk gaze. And this is what I saw. The dang thing was upright. It was jumping up and down. Red, white and blue flares emerged from it. Strains of "Stars and Stripes Forever" thrilled the air.

I knew what was going on.

The Great Gatsby and choral contingent were giving me a standing ovation.